THE BROKEN LEG OF DOOM

PAMELA BUTCHART

Look out for:

BABY ALIENS GOT MY TEACHER!

THE SPY WHO LOVED SCHOOL DINNERS

MY HEADTEACHER IS A VAMPIRE RAT!

ATTACK OF THE DEMON DINNER LADIES

TO WEE OR NOT TO WEE!

THERE'S A WEREWOLF IN MY TENT!

THE PHANTOM LOLLIPOP MAN!

THERE'S A YETI IN THE PLAYGROUND!

ICARUS WAS RIDICULOUS

First published in the UK in 2021 by Nosy Crow Ltd
The Crow's Nest, 14 Baden Place,
Crosby Row, London, SE1 1YW

Nosy Crow and associated logos are trademarks and/or registered
trademarks of Nosy Crow Ltd.

ISBN: 978 1 78800 787 0

A CIP catalogue record for this book will be available from the British Library.

Printed and bound in Great Britain by Clays Ltd, Elcograf S.p.A.

Papers used by Nosy Crow are made from wood grown in sustainable forests.

3 5 7 9 10 8 6 4

www.nosycrow.com

Contents

Bad Things Always Happen in Threes

I **KNEW** something bad was going to happen as **SOON** as we arrived at the hospital.

And I knew it because my mum says that bad things always happen in **THREES**. And **TWO** bad things had already happened that day because Jodi made us all do **EXTREME**

1

DANCING (which is when you dance as FAST as you can for as LONG as you can) and Maisie had got dizzy and fallen and broken her LEG. And then when we were in Jodi's mum's car following the ambulance to the hospital, I reached into my bag to get my **TWIX** because I was **STARVING** after all the dancing but it was **GONE**. And that's when I remembered that I'd already eaten it on my way to school.

So anyway, when we got to the hospital, I got a **WEIRD FEELING**. And it was because of the **CREEPY STATUE** in the entrance. And the **WEIRD SHAPE** of Maisie's **LEG** under the blanket. And the **STRANGE BOY** with the **FEATHER** in his hat.

But it was when we found out about the **CURSE** that we **KNEW**.

Maisie and her **LEG** were in

DEEP
TROUBLE.

Dancing Injury to the Right Leg

When we arrived at the hospital Jodi's mum parked the car and Zach yelled, "There's the ambulance. Look!" So I looked and that's when I saw the ambulance doors BURST open and Jodi came rushing out, pulling Maisie's stretcher behind her.

Jodi had REFUSED to come with us in the car to the hospital because she said she needed to stay with Maisie. And the paramedics had let her because Jodi told them she was Maisie's GUARDIAN because Maisie's mum wasn't there yet and that Maisie NEEDED HER and also that she would CHAIN herself to Maisie's stretcher IF NEED BE.

So me and Zach and Jodi's mum RAN after Maisie's stretcher into the

ACCIDENT AND EMERGENCY

bit of the hospital and up to the reception desk.

And before the paramedics could even say ONE WORD Jodi shouted,

"FEMALE.
AGED EIGHT YEARS,
FIVE AND A HALF MONTHS.
DANCING INJURY TO
THE RIGHT LEG.
POTENTIALLY BROKEN
IN NUMEROUS PLACES."

And as SOON as Jodi said that, Maisie SCREAMED at the top of her LUNGS and

everyone in the waiting room GASPED and the receptionist covered her ears with her hands because Maisie's scream is MEGA LOUD.

That's when one of the doctors came running over to see what was wrong. But then all of a sudden Maisie stopped screaming MID-SCREAM and closed her eyes and went COMPLETELY STILL.

So that's when I explained that Maisie had FAINTED from SHOCK because of what Jodi had just said and that it happened all the time. And that she'd wake up in a minute and need a Ribena and probably a Twix too,

and that I had some Ribena but that I didn't have a Twix. And then I explained about the TWIX THING and bad things happening in THREES.

But the doctor just stood there with a PANICKED look on his face and I started to worry because he didn't look that much older than my cousin Toby and he's still at secondary school. But then I noticed that he was wearing a hoody and carrying a bunch of grapes and that he was a visitor. And that he'd probably just come running over because of the noise Maisie was making.

Then Jodi started shouting for a

STETHOSCOPE so she could check Maisie's

VITAL ORGANS.

And a nurse appeared and said that she was going to take Maisie behind a little curtain to do an EXAMINATION and that we should all wait in the WAITING AREA, especially Jodi. And then she gave Jodi a bit of a LOOK so we went.

So me and Jodi and Zach sat down on the seats nearest to the little curtain and Jodi's mum said she was nipping outside to phone Maisie's mum again and that we should STAY EXACTLY WHERE WE WERE. But as soon as she left, Zach got up and said that he was going to find a vending machine so he could get a Twix and Jodi said, "How can you think of your STOMACH at a time like this, Zach?!"

And Zach said that he WASN'T thinking of his stomach and that he was thinking of MAISIE'S stomach, actually. And Jodi said, "Oh. Sorry."

And then she started crying and I got a SHOCK because Jodi NEVER cries. Not even the time she got her fingers jammed in the assembly-hall doors and they went PURPLE.

Then she said that it was ALL HER FAULT and that it should be HER LEG in hospital and that she was NEVER GOING TO DANCE AGAIN.

And it sort of WAS Jodi's fault because the dancing had been her idea (and even when we'd said we didn't want to do it she'd still made us because she said she'd already moved the furniture and made a

PLAYLIST).

But I didn't say any of that because Jodi was obviously feeling

MEGA GUILTY.

So I just patted her back a bit. And so did Zach.

And I said, "It's not your fault. Maisie's going to be OK. Don't worry."

But to be honest, I just said that to make Jodi feel better. Because I didn't know if Maisie WAS going to be OK. Because I had seen the WEIRD SHAPE of Maisie's LEG

under the blanket and it didn't look normal at ALL. And that's when Jodi's mum came back in and said, "What happened? Where's Maisie?"

And we all spun round and saw that the little curtain was OPEN and that Maisie and her leg were GONE.

The GIANT Leg Cast!

Once Jodi stopped screaming, the nurse explained to us that Maisie had been taken for an X-RAY on her leg and that she was perfectly SAFE and that she definitely hadn't been KIDNAPPED and that Jodi shouldn't have screamed that.

Then she asked Jodi's mum to fill out some forms and said that Maisie would be taken to

WARD 13

after her X-RAY. And that's when I heard Zach do a GULP and I knew that it was because Maisie is TERRIFIED of the number 13.

Like the time we went to the cinema for my birthday and Maisie wouldn't sit in her seat because it was NUMBER 13. We all tried to switch seats with her but she wouldn't let us because she said the seat was not just

UNLUCKY but probably DEADLY so she just had to sit on my knee the whole time because there weren't any more seats next to each other.

So anyway, we all rushed along the hospital corridor to get to

WARD 13.

And we went up loads of stairs and along another corridor and then up MORE stairs and that's when we realised that we were LOST.

Zach said that we should just keep going

the way that **HE** was suggesting because his mum used to **WORK** there but Jodi's mum said she thought we should get in the lift so we did.

But then we had to come out again because no one knew what level

WARD 13

was on so we didn't know which button to press. So that's when Jodi's mum said that she was going back down to the reception to ask for directions and told us to wait where we were until she got back and then

she disappeared down the stairs.

That's when Zach said that the only reason he'd got LOST was because the hospital was HUNDREDS of years old and had TWISTY BITS and SECRET DOORS and CONFUSING BITS and also that they must have MOVED

WARD 13

from where it used to be.

I just nodded and didn't say anything because I was exhausted from all the stairs and I was just about to sit down on the floor when Jodi said, **"SHHHH!"**

And then her eyes went wide and she put one finger over her lips to show us we weren't allowed to talk and her other hand in the air to show us that this was SERIOUS.

And that's when I GASPED because I could hear it TOO. It was Maisie screaming somewhere in the distance.

And that's when Jodi yelled, **"THIS WAY! FOLLOW ME!"**

So we did.

Maisie's screams got louder and louder as we ran along the corridor so we knew that we were DEFINITELY going in the right direction.

And when we got to the end of the corridor there was a huge door that said

WARD 13.

That's when Jodi said, "Here we go!"

And I knew that she'd said it because we had

NO IDEA

what to expect when we saw Maisie because

she was screaming REALLY LOUDLY.

Jodi took a deep breath and pushed the door with two hands.

But it wouldn't open.

Then Zach said, "There's a buzzer." And he pressed it.

But the buzzer didn't buzz. It made a weird CRACKLING sound instead, like its batteries were one hundred years old or something.

So Jodi tried to push the door open again but it still wouldn't budge.

Then, all of a sudden, a really far-away-sounding voice said, "Can I help you?"

And I jumped because I wasn't expecting

it and also because the voice sounded a bit CREEPY.

And Jodi yelled,

"YES! LET ME IN! I'M MAISIE'S MUM!"

I looked at Zach and Zach looked at me because even though Jodi looks the oldest out of all of us she is actually the youngest and I was pretty sure the doctors and nurses weren't going to believe that she was Maisie's mum.

But there obviously wasn't a hidden camera in the buzzer because all of a sudden there was a loud CLUNKING SOUND and the crackling voice said, "Come in."

So Jodi pushed the door again and it opened and as SOON as we stepped inside the ward I saw a creepy display on the wall about BANDAGES and I gasped!

And Zach asked me if I was OK so I just pointed to the display and he nodded because he obviously thought it was creepy too.

Then all of a sudden Jodi grabbed my hand and said, "She's stopped."

And I stopped looking at the display and that's when I realised that I couldn't hear screaming any more. So we ran over to where there were two rows of beds and looked around but we couldn't see Maisie in any of them. So we ran over to the next bay of beds. But we couldn't find her anywhere!

Then suddenly a voice said, "Are you looking for the Screaming Girl?"

And we turned and saw a boy sitting up in one of the beds and he was wearing a hat with a feather in it.

So I said yes because he was obviously talking about Maisie.

And the boy said, "She's over there next to the window. The nurses had to pull the curtain all the way round her bed to stop her from screaming."

So we all rushed up and Jodi was just about to pull back the curtain when I grabbed her arm to stop her because I was worried that she would give Maisie a fright.

Then I whispered, "Maisie? It's us. Can we come in?"

But there was no reply.

And then a voice said, "I think she's sleeping."

And I **JUMPED** because I had no idea the boy from the bed had followed us up to the curtain and was standing right behind us.

So Jodi pulled back the curtain really slowly and that's when we all

GASPED

because Maisie was lying in bed wearing headphones and an eye mask and her leg was being held up in the air by a rope thing and she had a

MASSIVE

CAST on it!

That's when a nurse appeared and asked us who we were and where Maisie's mum was.

So I looked at Jodi and Jodi did her most **PROFESSIONAL FACE** and stood up straight and said, "I am Maisie's **LEGAL GUARDIAN**."

The nurse looked a bit confused because Jodi obviously wasn't old enough to be someone's **GUARDIAN** so that's when I explained that we were with Jodi's mum and that she'd be here in a minute.

The nurse gave us a bit of a **LOOK** and then eventually nodded and told us to take a seat.

Then as she was leaving, she suddenly stopped and turned back to face us and said, "But whatever you do, **PLEASE** don't wake her up."

And I noticed that the nurse's eyes went a bit **WIDE** as she said it and that she looked a bit scared and I knew that it was probably because she didn't want Maisie to wake up and start screaming the hospital down again.

So we all sat down quietly around Maisie's bed and Jodi closed the curtain again to give us **PRIVACY**.

I really wanted to hold Maisie's little hand like I'd seen people do on **TV** when someone is in hospital but I didn't want her to wake up and get a fright.

That's when Jodi said, "I can't believe this is happening. This is **SERIOUS**. I just want to get her home and look after her ASAP."

Then Jodi said that as soon as Maisie was allowed to go home, she was going to ask her mum if she could go and live at Maisie's house for a while so she could look after her and do things like help her get out of bed in the morning and read all her favourite books to her and help her cut the right legs off all her trousers so they'd fit.

And that's when we heard a voice say, "Can I come in?" And I looked up and saw that the boy was back and that he was peeking around the curtain.

I looked at Jodi and she looked at me and I knew that we were both thinking the same thing and that the thing was that this boy was a bit strange because he kept sort of creeping up on us and also because of the hat.

So we said that it was OK for him to come in and he came in and stood next to Maisie's cast and STARED at it and that's when I saw that he was wearing school trousers under his hospital gown and massive slippers that looked like dogs' heads.

I wasn't sure how old he was but he looked a bit like he'd be in the year below us if he was at our school.

The boy pointed to Maisie's cast and said, "That's the biggest one I've ever seen. And I've seen a LOT."

Then the boy put his hands on his hips and did a long sigh and said, "Do you mind if I sit down?"

So I jumped up and gave him my chair because I was worried that he needed to sit down because he wasn't feeling well.

The boy sat down and leaned back in the chair and put his hands behind his head and said, "So. The name's Seb. You won't find anyone that's been here as long as I have.

So if you have any questions about anything just ask me, OK? I know everything there is to know about this place."

That's when Jodi got a bit of a weird look on her face and I could just TELL that she didn't trust Seb (because it takes Jodi AGES to trust people because she is a very SUSPICIOUS person).

And then she said, "Thanks. But we can just ask one of the nurses if we need to know something."

And that's when Seb did a bit of a laugh and shook his head at Jodi.

And then he leaned forward and said,

"You're better to ask ME, OK? I know things the nurses DON'T.

The **REAL STUFF**.

The **SECRETS**."

And then he leaned back again and crossed his legs and did a bit of a **SMIRK**.

So Jodi crossed her arms and said, "Like what?"

And that's when Seb said, "Oh, I don't think you're ready to hear it yet. I'm not sure you could handle it.

It's **BIG**."

And I could **TELL** that Jodi was getting **MEGA ANNOYED** but that she wasn't saying anything like she usually would if someone else was irritating her (like annoying Gary Petrie from our school). And I knew that the reason she wasn't saying anything was because she was worried Seb might be **SERIOUSLY UNWELL.**

So that's when I said, "Seb. We can handle it. **TRUST ME.**"

Because Seb obviously had

NO IDEA

about all the stuff that we'd had to deal with

at our school like

FRENCH SPIES and

WEREWOLVES and

DEMON DINNER LADIES.

So that's when Seb leaned forward and said, "OK. Well … I overheard what you said about Maisie's leg being serious and you're RIGHT. It IS serious."

And then he said, "Wait right there," and he stood up and peeked round the curtain and said, "Just checking."

I had no idea what Seb was checking FOR but I was starting to get a bit freaked out because he obviously knew something about the hospital that we DIDN'T and I was getting the feeling that it DEFINITELY was going to be a BAD THING.

Then Seb sat back down and put both hands on his knees and said, "Well. I guess I should probably tell you all about

THE

CURSE."

And then all of a sudden there was a

SCREAM.

The CURSE!

At first I thought the screaming was coming from Maisie until I noticed that she was still lying quietly with her eye mask on.

Zach jumped up and pulled back the curtain and that's when we saw Maisie's mum standing at the nurses' station with Jodi's mum and she looked **WILD**.

One of the nurses was trying to calm her down but it obviously wasn't working because Maisie's mum was still screaming and everyone was staring at her.

Zach rushed over and grabbed Maisie's mum's arm and pointed at us and that's when Maisie's mum saw me and Jodi and started rushing towards us.

I looked at Jodi and before I could even say a word Jodi grabbed the curtain and pulled it so it draped over Maisie's massive cast.

Maisie's mum ran over to Maisie and

grabbed her head and started kissing her all over her face and saying,

"MY POOR ANGEL WINGS!"

That's when Maisie took her eye mask off and gave her mum a big hug, and while they were doing that, I helped Jodi tuck the curtain in a bit better around Maisie's leg so Maisie's mum couldn't see the cast.

But then the kissing stopped and Maisie's mum turned and saw the weird LEG

CURTAIN THING that we'd made and before we could say a word she pulled the curtain off and saw Maisie's giant leg and fainted on the spot.

As soon as the doctors and nurses had taken Maisie's mum away on the stretcher we all

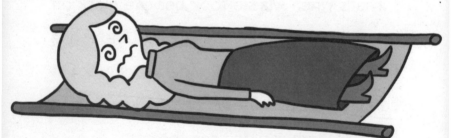

sat on Maisie's bed and held her hand and asked her how she was feeling.

That's when Maisie said that she was OK and that it didn't hurt as much any more and that she wanted us to sign her cast.

I couldn't BELIEVE how brave Maisie was being because I thought she was going to

FREAK OUT

when she woke up and saw her MASSIVE LEG hanging in the air, but she didn't.

That's when Jodi gave me a bit of a WORRIED LOOK and then she looked at Maisie and said, "Maisie. You don't understand what's happened."

And Maisie said that she did understand what had happened and that what had happened was that Jodi had made her do dancing and that she'd fallen and broken her leg because of it and now she was in hospital.

And that's when Jodi's face went a bit red and she stopped saying stuff about Maisie not knowing what was going on because she obviously did.

I could tell that Maisie was a bit annoyed at Jodi and that Jodi was feeling really guilty so that's when I tried to change the subject a bit and asked Maisie about the headphones.

And that's when Maisie smiled and passed them to me and I put them on for a second and heard loads of WHALE SOUNDS.

That's when Maisie told us that one of the ñurses had given them to her and that they had loads of sounds on them that you could choose from like

WHALE SONGS and

RAIN and SOUNDS OF

THE RAINFOREST.

Maisie **LOVES**

whales, especially humpback whales, so I knew that must have been what calmed her down and stopped her from screaming.

Maisie told us to try the headphones out so I put them back on and pressed the **RAINFOREST SOUNDS** button but it wasn't very relaxing and it was actually a bit **STRESSFUL** because it started with just one monkey but then after a minute there were **LOADS** of monkeys and they were all screaming.

So I took the headphones off and that's when I heard a voice right behind me say, "I can't believe it."

And I gasped and turned around and saw that Seb was standing there again.

I was just about to tell him off a bit for sneaking up on people because it was really getting on my nerves now but then I saw the look on his face. And the look on Jodi's face. And Zach's face. But Maisie didn't have a look on her face because her eyes were shut and her head was slumped to the side because she'd fainted.

And that's when I knew that I must have

missed something when I was listening to all the monkeys. And that it must have been something

BIG.

And then Zach said, "Are you sure?"

And Seb nodded his head and said, "I'm sure. It went in there."

And then he pointed to Maisie's cast.

I had

NO IDEA

what had gone inside Maisie's cast and I thought it must have been a FLY or something because there wasn't much space at all between her leg and the cast.

But then Jodi said, "I don't believe you."

And Seb said, "Well, you'd BETTER. Because this is REAL. I saw it with my own EYES."

And I couldn't believe that everyone knew what it was that had gone inside Maisie's

leg cast except for me or that I hadn't asked yet but it was one of those situations where everything goes really fast and it feels much faster than real life.

And that's when I eventually managed to say, "What? What went inside?! I had the monkeys in my ears!"

And that's when Seb put his hand on my shoulder and said,

"THE CURSE."

But then Jodi stood up and said that it was time for Seb to go and that he was talking

NONSENSE and that curses didn't even **EXIST**.

And that's when Maisie's eyes

SHOT OPEN

and she sat up and started yelling, "My leg! Something's happening. My **LEG**!!!"

And Seb looked at us and said, "See. I told you."

But Jodi HATES Eggs!

The next morning felt like the **LONGEST** morning **EVER**.

I couldn't concentrate on **ANYTHING** our teacher, Miss Jones, was saying because I kept thinking about Maisie being in the hospital without us and her broken leg and

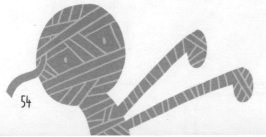

the CURSE that had sneaked into her CAST and was making her leg all ITCHY. And it didn't help that Jodi kept asking me what time it was every thirty seconds and asking me if I was SURE my watch wasn't broken.

Then at lunchtime the dinner ladies served Maisie's

FAVOURITE DESSERT,

pink custard with ice cream, and that's when Jodi actually THREW her tray on to the floor

and shouted,

"I CAN'T TAKE
THIS ANY MORE!"

Because Jodi gets really UPSET and ANGRY sometimes and she gets told off a LOT about it.

So I picked up the tray and put it back on top of the other trays. And I was glad that it was empty and that the dinner ladies hadn't seen Jodi throw it because they would have gone

MAD.

They already don't like us because they know we hate loads of their food (especially the shepherd's pie) and they don't like that we started a PETITION about getting it BANNED and they also don't like that it got LOADS of signatures and that some of the signatures were from TEACHERS.

So anyway, I grabbed Jodi's arm and pulled her out of the dining hall before she had a full-blown Jodi Tantrum because we'd already been sent to the head teacher's office that week and I didn't want to get sent back. (I don't have time to explain why just now but it had to do with starting our

own hairdresser's in the playground at break and Jodi giving Gary Petrie a **MOHICAN**.)

So I pulled Jodi along the bottom corridor and all the way to The Den (which is a secret room under the stairs that lead up the boys' toilets that only we know about).

Me and Jodi sat on one of the upturned buckets we use as chairs and Zach locked the door behind us because we have the only key.

And as soon as the door was locked Jodi said, "I don't think I'll be able to COPE if Maisie has a broken leg AND a curse!"

Jodi was obviously feeling really upset and GUILTY so that's when I knew that I was going to have to be in charge of the

and that it was going to be up to ME to start a PLAN about Maisie's LEG CURSE.

So I sat down and pulled up the floorboard and took out the **MINI WHITE BOARD** we accidentally stole and the **GOOD PENS** because that's where we keep everything so if anyone ever finds our den they won't find all our secret plans.

And then I said, "**OK**. What do we know about the curse so far?"

And Zach said that we knew that there was a

at the hospital and that it had gone inside Maisie's cast.

So I wrote:

> # SEB SAYS THERE'S A CURSE ON WARD 13. THE CURSE IS NOW INSIDE MAISIE'S LEG CAST.

And then I didn't write any more because we didn't know anything else.

So that's when Jodi said that we should come to her house for tea and use her mum's laptop to do RESEARCH.

And then she went a bit quiet and I looked and saw that she was staring at the bucket Maisie usually sits on.

So that's when I put the white board down and stood up and said, "OK. Let's DO this!"

And Zach and Jodi both gave me a bit of a weird look because they didn't realise what I was doing.

So that's when I stuck my arm out in front of me and said, "If we can deal with demons and vampire rats then we can deal with a curse. We can save Maisie. I KNOW we can... LET'S DO THIS!"

And then Zach jumped up and put his hand on top of my hand said, "Let's do this."

And I said, "Sorry, Zach. I didn't hear that. What did you *saaay*??"

Even though I obviously **HAD** heard him and I just wanted him to say it **LOUDER** so that Jodi would get up and focus on the **INVESTIGATION** and stop being sad and start being more Jodi-like.

And Zach smiled a bit and said, **"LET'S DO THIS!"**

And then Jodi stood up and slapped her hand on top of ours and yelled, **"LET'S DO THIS!"**

After school, me and Zach went to Jodi's house for our tea and to do research before going to visit Maisie in the hospital that evening.

But when we arrived, Jodi opened the door and said, "We're leaving. My mum says we can have tea at the hospital."

I didn't really want to eat HOSPITAL FOOD plus Jodi had said earlier that her mum was making CHICKEN SURPRISE for tea which I LOVE because the surprise is that she hides CHEESE and PEPPERONI inside the chicken breast and it's DELICIOUS and

I didn't think they'd have anything like that at the hospital. But I didn't say anything because Jodi obviously wanted to go and she already had her coat on.

Then when we arrived at the hospital Jodi did a huge sigh of RELIEF and said, "Thank goodness we're here!"

And that's when I noticed that Jodi was clutching something TIGHT in her hand. So I asked her what it was and she looked at the back of her mum's head and then gave me the WIDE EYES which I knew meant she'd

tell us once we were inside and her mum couldn't hear.

So we got out of the car and followed Jodi's mum into the hospital. And when we walked into the main entrance I saw that there was ANOTHER display about BANDAGES and a banner thing that said THE HISTORY OF THE BANDAGE.

And I was just about to ask what all the BANDAGE STUFF was about when I saw a CREEPY STATUE THING with bits of OLD BANDAGES hanging off it and I GASPED.

I looked to see if Jodi and Zach had

noticed the **CREEPY STATUE** but they hadn't because they had gone ahead of me and they were walking into the café.

And that's when I forgot all about the creepy statue because I thought we were having dinner with Maisie in the ward not at a café by ourselves! So I rushed over and that's when Jodi explained that we weren't allowed to visit the ward until 6pm and that we were having our dinner in the café first.

So I asked Jodi why we couldn't have just had dinner at her house before we came since we weren't even allowed to go to the ward yet.

And that's when Jodi's eyes went WIDE again and she said, "We need to be ON SITE in case something happens."

And then she grabbed a tray and put a banana and an egg sandwich on it and that's when I knew that there was something SERIOUSLY WRONG because Jodi HATES eggs.

So we all sat down and Jodi unpeeled her banana and started eating it and I couldn't take my eyes off her because she was eating it REALLY weirdly and really FAST. And I couldn't even remember the last time I'd seen Jodi eat a banana!

So I waited until Jodi's mum went to the toilet and then I said, "OK. What's going ON?!"

And that's when Jodi's eyes went wide and she took the rolled-up piece of paper that she'd been clutching out of her coat pocket and said, "I need to show you something. We have a problem.

A **BIG** problem."

And Zach did a gulp.

The CURSED Bus!

I felt a bit dizzy after reading the piece of paper.

I looked at Zach to see how he was feeling because I had read it first and then handed it to him. And then I'd drunk Jodi's mum's cup of tea to try to calm down because I was

FREAKING OUT

a bit and my mum ALWAYS has a cup of tea when she's stressed about something. Like when she has a work DEADLINE or when the CREDIT CARD BILL comes or every time Gran and Granddad arrive half an hour early for dinner and Mum hasn't even put the potatoes on yet.

So anyway, I looked at Zach and he was STARING at the piece of paper and his left EYE was TWITCHING a bit. And I wasn't surprised at all about the staring OR the

TWITCHING because Jodi had a NEW list of information about CURSES. And it was BAD. And that's when I realised why Jodi had been acting so strangely.

Then Jodi said, "I asked my mum about curses as soon as I got home because I remembered that she used to watch this programme about them and it had MUMMIES in it."

And that's when Zach's eyes almost POPPED out of his head because Zach is TERRIFIED of mummies and he actually locked himself in the toilet when the Year 6s did a MUSICAL about ANCIENT EGYPT and he refused to come out until it was over.

So anyway, Jodi took a really deep breath and then she got a SERIOUS LOOK on her face and said, "If Seb's right about there being a curse on WARD 13 and it HAS gone into Maisie's leg cast then we have to do something

ASAP."

Then she opened her eyes even WIDER than they already were and said, "And there's ZERO time to WASTE."

And she was RIGHT because the list said:

CURSES

1. If you're cursed, LOADS of bad things happen to you (it's like having loads of BAD LUCK or being DOOMED)
2. People AND things can be cursed (even a bus)
3. Sometimes people who were cursed in Ancient Egypt got SPOTS all over their body and one man even grew a TAIL
4. If you disturb an ancient MUMMY'S TOMB a CURSE will be released
5. Ancient Egyptians believed that the CURSE OF THE MUMMY was DEADLY

So that's when I asked Jodi about the CURSED BUS thing and she said that her mum told her that she used to get a bus to college every Tuesday when she was learning to be a hairdresser and that EVERY SINGLE TUESDAY the bus broke down and she'd have to walk the rest of the way to college and that the bus was obviously

CURSED.

Then Zach said, "Maybe it wasn't the bus

that was cursed. Maybe it was someone ON the bus that was cursed."

And Jodi spun her head round to face Zach and said, "Are you trying to say that my mum's cursed or something?! Because she's **NOT!**"

And I got a shock because Jodi didn't say it very nicely and it was a bit of an

OVERREACTION.

But then Jodi told Zach that she was sorry and that she was just really worried about Maisie in case it was a MUMMY'S CURSE.

And that's when I remembered all the displays about **BANDAGES** and the **WEIRD STATUE THING** that had been wrapped in **BANDAGES** and I **GASPED** and said, "It is!

It **IS** a

MUMMY'S CURSE!"

And Jodi and Zach stared at me.

So that's when I took a **DEEP BREATH** and explained about the displays and the statue and that the hospital must have something to do with ANCIENT MUMMIES and that maybe they STUDIED them here hundreds of years ago or something and accidentally set a mummy's curse LOOSE.

Zach put his head in his hands and I knew that it was because he didn't want the MUMMY THING to be true. So I looked at Jodi and she put both of her hands FLAT on the table and STARED at me with WIDE EYES and said, "If there's a mummy's curse still in the hospital then there might still be an actual MUMMY."

And that's when Zach yelled, "WHAT?! NO WAY! I CAN'T DEAL WITH THIS!!!"

But then Jodi's mum came back from the toilet and asked Zach why he was shouting. But Zach didn't answer because he was obviously in SHOCK and Jodi's mum didn't even notice because she was too busy looking inside the little teapot and trying to figure out what had happened to all her tea.

My head was absolutely SPINNING and it was because Jodi had just said that there might be an actual ancient MUMMY in the hospital! And because Zach was bouncing both his legs up and down with STRESS. And Jodi was STARING into the air like she was

and eating her egg sandwich even though she HATES eggs.

And then all of a sudden there was an announcement and it said:

"ALL AVAILABLE STAFF TO

WARD 13.

ALL AVAILABLE
STAFF TO WARD 13.
RIGHT AWAY!"

And I GASPED.

And Jodi dropped her egg sandwich on the floor.

Because that was

MAISIE'S WARD!!!

SPRINKLERS!

Before I could even **BLINK**, Jodi had **VAULTED** over the café barrier and was running **FULL SPEED** across the hospital.

Jodi's mum grabbed her bag and told us to leave our food and started running after her and **YELLING** at her to **SLOW DOWN**.

But Jodi **DIDN'T** slow down.

So me and Zach ran after them both but we couldn't keep up because Jodi is SUPER FAST and so is her mum!

That's when Zach grabbed my arm and said, "LIFT!"

And I looked and saw that there were people getting into the lift and that the doors were still open. So we RAN as fast as we could towards the lift and it was TOTALLY STRESSFUL because just as we were getting close the doors started to CLOSE.

So I waved my hands in the air and shouted,

"WAIT FOR US! KEEP THEM OPEN!"

But the people in the lift weren't paying attention and the doors just kept on closing.

And then all of a sudden, Zach started running faster than I have EVER seen him run. And it was like watching someone in the OLYMPICS or something!

And then he jumped up in the air and kicked his LEG out into a HIGH KICK and flew towards the lift and stuck his foot inside just as the doors were closing!

And I actually SCREAMED when he did it because I was SURE that he was going to end up in Ward 13 in the bed next to Maisie with a CRUSHED FOOT! But he didn't. Because the doors froze where they were and then started to open again!

That's when Zach jumped up off the floor and he had a HUGE smile on his face and he said, "IT WORKED!"

And I burst out LAUGHING because it HAD worked and also because I think I was in a bit of SHOCK because I thought I'd just watched my best friend get his FOOT

CRUSHED.

So we ran into the lift and we were totally out of breath and everyone was STARING at us with their mouths wide open because they probably thought we were MARTIAL ARTS EXPERTS or something.

I smiled at everyone to try to be polite while Zach reached up and pressed FLOOR 6 because that's what floor Ward 13 is on. But no one really smiled back which was a bit rude but I knew that it was probably because we'd given them a FRIGHT.

Then when we got to Floor 6 I said thanks to everyone in the lift even though they hadn't kept the door open or pressed the button for us because it felt like the right thing to do.

Then suddenly Zach yelled, "THERE!" and pointed and I saw Jodi's ponytail disappear around the corner at the bottom of the corridor.

So we RAN after her and when we got to the end the big door was still open so we didn't have to buzz the buzzer and we just ran in.

And to be honest with you I hadn't really known WHAT to expect when we arrived because of the URGENT

ANNOUNCEMENT.

But I definitely didn't expect

THIS.

It was CHAOS. All the nurses and doctors were running around and there was loads of SCREAMING and SHOUTING. And everyone was SOAKING WET because the SPRINKLERS were on FULL BLAST.

Me and Zach stood there with our mouths WIDE OPEN and I knew for a FACT that my mouth was wide open because I could TASTE the sprinkler water.

Then all of a sudden someone was standing in front of us with their hood up.

At first I thought it was Jodi because I couldn't see very well because the normal ward lights weren't on and there was a weird, dull red light instead, like we were in a SUBMARINE or something.

I looked at Zach but I couldn't really see his face EITHER because his hair was SOAKED and it was hanging down over his nose.

And then all of a sudden the HOODED FIGURE grabbed our hands and I just KNEW that it wasn't Jodi because that's not what Jodi's hands FEEL like!

"Follow me if you want to live!"

I was literally about to scream the WHOLE HOSPITAL down when I saw that the hooded figure was wearing massive DOG SLIPPERS.

That's when I yelled, "Seb?! What's going ON?!"

And Seb said, "Follow me if you want to LIVE."

And then he pulled us along the ward, past loads of nurses and doctors who were rushing around covering their heads with their hands and shouting about the water.

I could barely see a THING because of the water and WEIRD LIGHT but then all of a sudden Seb pulled us into a small room and the water stopped and Jodi was standing there.

Jodi shut the door and asked us if we were OK and we nodded that we were. And that's when I looked around and saw loads of toilet roll on shelves and a mop and bucket in the corner and I realised that we must be in a cleaning cupboard. And it made me think of The Den at school and I wanted to be there SO MUCH.

Seb wiped the water off his jacket and then took his hood down and put his hat with the feather back on. But before he put his hat on I noticed that he had a red rash across the top of his forehead.

I was about to ask Seb if he was OK when he said, "You guys were lucky I found you all when I did or you'd be completely SOAKED. I saved your SKINS!"

And that's when Zach yelled, "No, you didn't! Why did you bring us here?! We need to get out NOW! We need to find the FIRE ESCAPE!!"

And that's when I GASPED because everything had happened so FAST with the NINJA HIGH-KICK and then SPRINKLERS and the HOODED FIGURE that I hadn't actually realised that the sprinklers being on meant there must be a FIRE!

I GRABBED Jodi and reached out to open the door. But Seb stood in front of me and said, "Stop! There's no fire. It's the CURSE!"

But I didn't CARE what Seb was saying

94

because I was SURE there must be a fire so I pushed him out of the way and ran out into the corridor and grabbed the first nurse I could see and yelled, "Where's the fire escape?!"

And that's when the nurse said that there WASN'T a fire and that the sprinklers were just MALFUNCTIONING AGAIN and that I should stay where I was until it stopped.

So I went back into the cupboard and closed the door and Seb said, "I told you. There's no fire alarm. It's just the sprinklers."

So I started to calm down a bit. But then I remembered something and I said, "What

about Maisie? Where is she? She'll be terrified out there!"

And I knew that I was **RIGHT** because Maisie **HATES** showers and she only has baths. And one time when we were on a school camping trip she **FREAKED OUT** when she found out that there weren't any baths in the **SHOWER BLOCK** and she ended up getting washed in a **BUCKET** because that's all there was and also because she's really small so she could fit.

So anyway, I was just about to go out and save Maisie when a little voice said, "I'm right here."

And I GASPED because the voice was coming from near my FEET.

I looked down and saw that Maisie was in the cupboard with us and that she was lying on the ground with a pillow under her MASSIVE leg cast. And I couldn't BELIEVE that I hadn't spotted her until now and that I hadn't actually STEPPED on her by mistake!

That's when Seb explained that he had carried Maisie from her bed to the cupboard just before the sprinklers

MALFUNCTIONED. And I noticed that Maisie wasn't wet like we were.

I got down on the ground and went up close to Maisie and asked how she was feeling and she said that she was fine and that she was glad she didn't get her cast wet because she'd already managed to get it signed by most of the doctors and nurses and that she didn't want the ink to run. And then she started smiling and pointing to a picture that one of the doctors had drawn for her of a HUMPBACK WHALE.

And I was a bit SHOCKED because usually Maisie is terrified of EVERYTHING and I

didn't understand why she wasn't more scared about the whole **SPRINKLER THING** and I definitely didn't understand why she wasn't freaking out about the **CURSE** because Seb had just mentioned it!

So that's when I asked Maisie if she was **OK** and told her that she didn't need to worry and that we had everything **UNDER CONTROL** (even though we definitely **DIDN'T** have everything under control because we didn't even have a **PLAN** yet and there was a curse inside Maisie's **BROKEN LEG!**).

And that's when I felt someone kick my leg and I looked up and saw that it was Jodi and

I was about to say, "Hey! That hurt!" when I realised that she was making her

and pointing at Maisie and then at her own EARS.

At first, I thought Jodi was maybe losing the plot a bit because she'd just eaten the first egg sandwich of her LIFE and she just kept pointing to her ears loads and then pointing to Maisie like she was POSSESSED or something! But then I noticed that Maisie had her HEADPHONES in her hand and that she must have been WEARING THEM when Seb had said that the sprinklers were CURSED and that she didn't actually KNOW about

THE CURSE yet.

So I forgave Jodi for the KICK and she knew that I had because I nodded at her and stopped screwing up my face and eyes like I had been.

That's when Seb did a long sigh and said, "Well … it looks like we might be stuck in here for a while. Last time this happened it

took **AGES** to fix. Just as well I hid **THIS** in here in case anything like that ever happened again."

We all watched as Seb pulled out a box from under one of the shelves and looked up at us with a **HUGE GRIN** on his face.

And then he said, "I've got Coke, Diet Coke, lemonade and sparkling water. I've also got KitKats, chocolate digestives, shortbread, a chocolate-chip flapjack and a banana. What does everyone want?"

We all stood there **STARING** at Seb as he picked all the cans of fizzy drinks and biscuits out of the box and lined them up neatly on

the floor.

Then Zach said, "I'll take a KitKat, please. And do you have any fresh orange juice?"

Seb stroked his chin for a bit with his fingers and then he said, "Let me just take a look in the back."

And then he got up and went over to the shelves and pulled out ANOTHER box and said, "I can offer you an apple juice. Would that be any good to you?"

Zach nodded that it would be and Seb threw it over and Zach caught it and smiled to himself because he hadn't dropped it.

Then Seb pulled something ELSE out of the box and smiled and said, "Anyone fancy a game?!"

And I looked and saw that it was MONOPOLY. And I had

NO IDEA

what was going on or why Seb had a MINI SHOP with BOARD GAMES hidden in an old cleaning cupboard in a hospital!

Maisie clapped her hands with excitement as Seb started to set up the board.

And then he held out all the little SILVER

THINGS that you have to choose from when you play Monopoly and looked at Maisie and said, "Lady Maisie!" and then he did a bit of a bow thing at Maisie and she giggled.

Then he said, "Which one would you like to be?"

And that's when Maisie said that she didn't mind as long as it wasn't the SHOE because she wasn't going to be able to wear shoes or walk properly for a long time.

So that's when Seb closed his eyes and waved his other hand dramatically in the air for ages and said, "Let me see, let me see, let me SEE! I shall pick one at RANDOM

and hope it's one you like!"

And he winked at Maisie before closing his eyes and picking one of the silver things from his other hand. And then he held it out in front of Maisie.

And Maisie said, "The HAT! That's perfect! It reminds me of you."

And Seb smiled and took off his hat and did ANOTHER bow and I saw that he had a rash on the back of his head too.

That's when I felt someone pinch my arm and I turned and it was Jodi and she said, "Are they boyfriend and girlfriend now or something?!"

And I shrugged because I didn't really know **WHAT** was going on or why Seb had all these **HIDDEN SUPPLIES**.

And then all of a sudden the shouting outside the door stopped and everyone cheered and started clapping and Zach said, "The sprinklers must have stopped!"

And that's when I noticed that Seb looked a bit disappointed and I knew that it was probably because he'd just finished setting up the **MONOPOLY BOARD**.

Then Jodi whispered, "We need to get Maisie back to her bed and then ask Seb more about this curse."

And I nodded because I knew that we
DEFINITELY DID. Because if the curse
could make all the SPRINKLERS go off
then who KNEW what else it could do to
Maisie's leg!

Zach opened the cupboard door and
peeked outside and said, "It's definitely
stopped. The lights are back on now, too."

So Jodi said that we should all help get
Maisie up off the floor SLOWLY so we did.
And then Jodi and Zach lifted Maisie up
and took an arm and a leg each and I put a
cushion under Maisie's broken leg just to be
sure.

Then just as I was following them out Seb grabbed my arm and held me back and said, "You guys really need to be here EVERY DAY to keep an eye on the curse, OK?"

So I said that we would be and also that we needed to ask him more about the curse ASAP.

That's when Seb smiled and said, "You mean, like an interview?"

And it sort of WAS like an interview because we were doing an investigation.

So I said, "Yes. Can you do it when we get back to the ward?"

And Seb said that he could and he looked

really happy about it, which I thought was a bit weird because this was SERIOUS and pretty SCARY.

Then Seb held out his hand for me to shake and said, "Looking forward to it, Izzy. I'll wear my best hat!"

And that's when I noticed that he had a rash on his hand too. And then he must have noticed that I'd noticed because he pulled his hand away quickly and put it in his pocket.

Then all of a sudden Zach appeared back at the door with a weird look on his face and said, "Izzy, you'd better come. Quick."

The MUMMY'S Curse!

When we got back to the main bit of the ward, Maisie's mum was there and she looked TERRIBLE. Seb actually GASPED when he saw her and I'm not surprised because it looked like she'd been in a WAR or something!

Maisie's mum was sitting in one of the plastic chairs next to Jodi's mum and she had her legs up, hugging them and rocking backwards and forwards and she had loads of mascara running down her face.

Jodi's mum was trying to hold a COOL CLOTH up to her head to calm her down but it wasn't working and she would have been better just using the cloth to wipe her face instead.

I noticed that Maisie wasn't there and that's when Jodi said that one of the nurses had taken Maisie to the toilet in a wheelchair and that she'd tried to tell Maisie's mum that she

was just in the toilet but that Maisie's mum wouldn't listen.

Then all of a sudden Maisie appeared in the wheelchair and as SOON as Maisie's mum saw her she stopped rocking and LEAPT off the chair in ONE MOVE like a FLYING VAMPIRE or something!

Maisie's mum grabbed Maisie and started stroking her arms and her hair and her face and wailing, "I thought you'd DROWNED, my ANGEL WINGS!"

I didn't really think that it made sense that Maisie could have DROWNED because of the SPRINKLER WATER but I didn't say anything because that's just what Maisie's mum is like and she always OVERREACTS to everything.

Like the time Maisie got locked in the bathroom in her house for SEVEN minutes and Maisie's mum was so upset that she ended up taking all the doors off all the toilets so Maisie couldn't get locked in the toilet ever again. And it took her AGES because Maisie actually lives in a MANSION and there are

SIX TOILETS

in her house. And now when we're at Maisie's house I have to get Jodi to stand outside and make sure no one passes in the hallway and sees me or walks in while I'm on the toilet, which is really annoying.

So anyway, once Maisie's mum had calmed down and stopped saying the stuff about thinking Maisie had drowned and let Jodi's mum wipe her MASCARA FACE, the nurse said that we had to pack up Maisie's things and that Maisie had to MOVE WARDS for the night because everything in Ward 13 was soaking wet but that she could come back in the morning.

That's when Jodi asked the nurse if Maisie could maybe just come home for the night and that she'd take good care of her.

But before the nurse could even answer Seb shouted,

"NO!"

We all STARED at Seb because we had no idea why he'd shouted that.

And then Seb said, "I mean. I just mean, it's late. It's almost eight o'clock. It's better to stay here."

I looked at Jodi and she crossed her arms and narrowed her eyes at Seb and I knew that it was probably because she was annoyed at him for saying that because she wanted to take Maisie home.

That's when the nurse said that Maisie needed to stay in hospital until the doctor came to see her and that he had been on his way to see Maisie before the sprinklers went off and that he'd be back in the morning.

Then Jodi said, "So Maisie might get to come home tomorrow?"

And the nurse said that it was up to the doctor.

Then the nurse looked at Maisie's bed that looked AMAZING because her mum had covered it in FAIRY LIGHTS and STARS and TEDDIES. But then the nurse made a bit of a face and said, "Perhaps some of this can go home with you?"

That's when Maisie's mum said that it COULDN'T and that she'd only brought Maisie's ESSENTIALS. And that's when the nurse raised her EYEBROWS and looked at the GIANT HUMPBACK WHALE sitting on the chair.

But then Maisie noticed what the nurse was looking at and said, "But Francisco's my

most favourite thing

EVER!„

And that's when the nurse brought her eyebrows back down **RIGHT AWAY** and didn't say anything else about the whale and I knew that it was because she was scared Maisie was going to start **SCREAMING** again.

So I said that we'd help pack Maisie's stuff and take it to the new ward because I didn't think it was a good idea for the nurse to be helping because she hadn't noticed the other bags of stuff under Maisie's bed yet.

That's when Seb said, "Can you guys come over to my bed and help me pack up my stuff too?"

So we helped Maisie's mum for a bit and then we went over to help Seb.

But when we went over, Seb said that he didn't really need help because he didn't have much stuff and that he just wanted to start the INTERVIEW.

I felt bad for Seb when he said that because that's when I noticed that he didn't have any cards and gifts and stuff from home like Maisie had.

Jodi looked over to make sure Maisie wasn't listening and then she said, "OK. You need to tell us everything you know about the CURSE."

And that's when Seb said, "Well ... where to start!"

And then he jumped up on the bed and crossed his legs.

That's when Jodi said that he should start at the beginning and tell us everything about the curse and that she'd write it all down.

And that's when Seb said that the curse had been around as long as he had and that he'd been coming here for YEARS and that every time he came back to the ward the curse was more POWERFUL and more DANGEROUS.

And then he got a SERIOUS look on his face and said, "That means Maisie can't leave."

That's when Jodi raised her eyebrows and said, "What?!"

And Seb took a deep breath and said, "Well, at the moment the curse is trapped inside Maisie's leg cast, which is good."

And I couldn't BELIEVE that Seb had said that! So that's when I said that I didn't think it WAS good at ALL that the curse was trapped inside our friend's leg cast!

But then Seb shook his head and said that that wasn't what he'd meant and that what he'd meant was that as long as it was TRAPPED in Maisie's cast, it couldn't ESCAPE.

And then he sat down on the edge of his bed and said, "We need to keep the

curse trapped and find out more about it, like where it came from and why it's inside Maisie's leg cast and what it WANTS. And that might take weeks or even MONTHS."

But then Jodi said, "Or we need to BREAK the curse so it disappears altogether?"

But then Seb laughed a bit and shook his head and said, "You can't BREAK a curse, Jodi. You don't even know anything about curses!"

And Jodi crossed her arms and said, "I DO, actually."

And Seb looked a bit SHOCKED when Jodi said that.

125

And he said, "Oh. Um. Well." And then he didn't say anything else for a bit and it was probably because he felt a bit silly.

Then Seb said, "OK. What do you know?"

And that's when I looked at Jodi and Jodi looked at Zach and Zach looked at me because that's what we do when we are trying to decide if we should share our INFORMATION with people who are not us when we are investigating all the weird stuff that seems to happen to us.

And that's when I took a DEEP BREATH and said, "We think it might be an ancient mummy's curse."

And then I explained about Jodi's research and also about the hospital having loads of displays about THE HISTORY OF THE BANDAGE and that MUMMIES are wrapped in bandages and that mummies might have been STUDIED here hundreds of years ago.

I looked at Zach and he was gripping the plastic bit at the bottom of Seb's bed and he had his eyes closed and was making a bit of a weird SQUEAKING sound.

Then I looked at Jodi and she had her fingers on her TEMPLES and was rubbing them round and round because that's the new thing she does now when she is

STRESSED.

And I could feel my heart beating really fast because I was freaking out about the MUMMY'S CURSE!

And that's when I noticed that Seb WASN'T freaking out. And that he didn't look SHOCKED or STRESSED and that he wasn't SQUEAKING or anything like that.

Then all of a sudden Seb's eyes went wide and he jumped off the bed and said, "Do you know what? I think you might be RIGHT about it being a MUMMY'S CURSE. That's so COOL!"

So that's when Jodi said that it definitely

WASN'T COOL or **FUN** and that this was a

SERIOUS INVESTIGATION

and that if he was going to be a part of it, he would have to be more **PROFESSIONAL**.

And that's when Seb looked over Jodi's shoulder and made a noise with his throat like you do when you're trying to get someone's attention. And we turned round and saw that Maisie was standing right behind us with the giant humpback whale under her arm.

And for a second I thought she'd overheard us but then she said, "Izzy, can you carry

Francisco for me, please?"

And she handed me her humpback whale.

Then just as we were all leaving the ward Seb whispered, "And by the way. I think I know where the mummy's curse came from. And I can SHOW YOU. Would lunchtime tomorrow work for you?"

And Zach GASPED.

And Jodi's eyes went WIDE.

And Seb smiled and said, "Is that professional enough for you?"

The Ransom Note

The next day was Saturday so we didn't have to go to school and my dad took us to see Maisie in the hospital instead.

Jodi made us leave the house ages before the hospital visiting hours started and she even made my dad go a different way in the car than he wanted to because she was sitting in the front seat and she kept saying that her mum knew how to get there quicker, over and over again, until he eventually gave in and let Jodi tell him which way to go.

When we got there, we went straight to the ward and pressed the buzzer but no one answered. So Jodi pressed it again and she kept her finger on it for ages.

That's when Zach said that we were **TWENTY SIX AND A HALF MINUTES** early because he got a new watch for his birthday and it's a **DIGITAL ONE** that doesn't have **HANDS** and it tells you the

exact time to the MILLISECOND.

So my dad said that we should go and get a cup of tea and come back later and also that Jodi should take her finger off the buzzer now.

But then all of a sudden the door clicked open and a nurse appeared and she looked STRESSED and she said, "Is one of you Izzy?!"

And I got a bit of a SHOCK because I wasn't expecting her to say that and I said, "I am. I'm Izzy."

And that's when the nurse let out a big sigh and closed her eyes and put her hand up to

her chest and said, "Oh, thank goodness! Come in! Come in!" and then she RUSHED me inside and up to Maisie's bed.

And that's when I saw that Maisie had the HEADPHONES on again and that her eyes were shut TIGHT and also that she was breathing into a PAPER BAG.

I turned and looked at Jodi and Zach because I thought that Maisie must have found out about the CURSE.

But then the nurse yelled, "Look Maisie! It's Izzy!"

And Maisie's eyes shot open and she pulled the paper bag away from her mouth and said, "Izzy! Where is he?! Please tell me that you know where he is, Izzy!"

I had **NO IDEA** what Maisie was talking about or who "he" was. And I was so confused that I turned and looked at Zach for a second just to double check he was definitely there in case she was talking about him.

Then Zach said, "Who? Seb?"

And that's when I looked around at the other beds but I couldn't see Seb anywhere.

Then suddenly Maisie yelled, **"I CAN'T LIVE WITHOUT HIM!"**

And that's when Jodi rushed forward and

put the paper bag back up to Maisie's mouth and told her to take DEEP BREATHS.

And then she said, "Seb's probably just better and he's gone home. And you definitely CAN live without him. We've only known him for two days!"

And I could just TELL by the way Jodi said what she said that she didn't really like Seb and I knew that it was probably because she liked to be the one who knew the most about what was going on and to be in charge.

But then Maisie started VIOLENTLY shaking her head and she was doing it so fast that her face looked all BLURRY and her pigtails were hitting Jodi in the FACE.

And then all of a sudden I

GASPED

because I realised what was going on.

And who "he" was.

And I got that weird SINKING feeling that you get sometimes when something goes wrong and you know that it's BAD.

REALLY bad.

Because something was missing.

And not just ANYTHING.

It was FRANCISCO.

I could tell that Jodi was getting

MEGA ANNOYED

at the nurses. And I knew that it was because she thought they weren't taking it SERIOUSLY enough about FRANCISCO

being **STOLEN** and the **MISSING PERSONS' REPORT**.

Because Jodi kept asking over and over again if the reason they wouldn't let her fill in a **MISSING PERSONS' FORM** was because it hadn't been twenty-four hours yet. And the nurses just kept **SIGHING** and saying that it wasn't **ANYTHING** to do with that and that it was to do with the missing person being a **TOY WHALE**.

And I actually thought Jodi's head might **EXPLODE** when one of the nurses suggested that we just go down to the gift shop and get Maisie **ANOTHER ONE**

because the hospital gift shop **OBVIOUSLY** wouldn't be able to help us because how many hospital gift shops have **GIANT HUMPBACK WHALE TEDDIES** called **FRANCISCO** who have had their tummy signed by someone **FAMOUS**?!

So I just told the nurse thank you very much and pulled Jodi away and into the **WAITING AREA** bit and made her take a seat.

And that's when Jodi said, "Izzy. I **NEED** to find that whale and get it back to Maisie. I **NEED** to."

And I nodded because I knew that Jodi felt like if she found Francisco then she wouldn't need to feel as guilty about Maisie and her broken leg.

So that's when I said that I needed to find him TOO because I'd actually been the last one to SEE HIM when I carried him down to Maisie's new ward the night before. And I knew that that was the reason Maisie was asking to see ME in case I'd put him somewhere she couldn't see or taken him home with me or something (which would be pretty hard because Francisco is HUGE and he's about half the size of Maisie).

That's when Jodi said, "OK. We're going to need to do this ourselves. Where's the last place you remember seeing him?"

Then she told me to wait while she went to get her notebook out of her bag.

So I sat down and shut my eyes and tried to remember EXACTLY where I'd put Francisco. And I was SURE that I'd sat him on the chair right next to Maisie's new bed so I couldn't see how he'd have gone missing unless someone moved him.

Then all of a sudden Jodi appeared and her eyes were MASSIVE.

And she said, "You need to come back over here. There's a message. It's about Francisco."

And then she didn't say anything else so I got up and followed her back over to the bay where Maisie was.

Maisie was SHAKING and Zach was trying to get her to drink RIBENA from a straw to calm her down but he couldn't get the straw in her mouth because of all the SHAKING.

So I asked to see the message and that's when Zach said, "It's not a message. It's a RANSOM NOTE."

And I looked at Jodi and she nodded.

So I asked to see it and I thought Jodi was going to pass it to me.

But she didn't.

She pointed at Maisie's leg cast.

And I
GASPED.

Whale-napped!

I couldn't believe it. I had to read the message about **FIFTY TIMES** before I eventually said,

"Is this really **HAPPENING?!**"

And Jodi said that it was DEFINITELY HAPPENING and that it was SERIOUS.

And she was RIGHT because the message on Maisie's cast said:

YOU MUST STAY HERE FOREVER IF YOU WANT TO SEE YOUR DOLPHIN AGAIN. FROM THE CURSE.

That's when I said I needed to sit down because I DID and also because everything felt like it was getting really

OUT OF CONTROL

with Maisie's broken LEG and the CURSE and now CREEPY MESSAGES appearing on Maisie's cast!

Jodi grabbed the curtain and pulled it all the way round Maisie's bed so no one could see in and then she said, "We need to have a secret meeting. NOW."

So we all pulled our chairs as close to Maisie's bed as we could and waited for Jodi to say something. And it took AGES because Jodi kept opening her mouth like she was about to say something and then closing it again. And she must have done that about five times before Zach said, "Jodi, are you OK?"

And that's when Jodi eventually said, "Yes. I mean, no. It's just...This doesn't make any sense. A CURSE wouldn't write a message on someone's leg! I don't even think curses CAN write."

Jodi got up and peeked round the curtain to make sure no one was listening to us and then she said, "I don't think it was the curse that wrote the message. I think it was someone else. A PERSON."

But then Zach shook his head and said that he didn't agree. And that he thought the message on Maisie's leg was the curse's way of COMMUNICATING with us.

Then Zach's EYES went WIDE and he said, "It makes perfect sense! The curse is trapped INSIDE the cast so that's why the message appeared on it. It's communicating with us from the inside. It's trying to tell us what it wants!"

Then Zach touched the message with

his finger and said, "The words probably appeared REALLY SLOWLY in the night while Maisie was sleeping. You probably wouldn't have been able to read it until the message SEEPED all the way through the cast."

So that's when I gave Zach a LOOK because he was OBVIOUSLY forgetting that Maisie was RIGHT THERE.

And then Zach said, "Sorry, Maisie. I know all the curse stuff is scary. Are you OK?"

But Maisie didn't answer because her EYES had gone all SWIRLY and she was moving her head in the weird way she always does right before she faints.

So we put loads of pillows around her head so she could have a little fainting nap as she does sometimes when things are too scary for her.

So anyway, that's when Jodi said, "Izzy, what do you think? Do you think it was the curse that wrote the note?"

And I didn't know if it was the CURSE communicating with us or if it was someone ELSE. But what I DID know was that the message was pretty clear. They wanted Maisie to stay in the hospital

⭐ FOREVER. ⭐

And Jodi must have been thinking the same thing because that's when she said, "Why would the curse want Maisie to stay here forever? That doesn't make sense."

That's when Zach said that maybe the curse just LIKED living inside Maisie leg. And I was really happy that Maisie was asleep when he said that because I don't think Maisie would be happy with a CURSE living in her leg for the rest of her life!

Jodi stood up and put her hands on her hips (which is what she does when she's about to say something BIG). But before she could open her mouth, Seb peeked his head round the curtain and said, "You ready to find out how the curse got here?"

Zach wouldn't stop **FIDGETING** so Jodi made him sit on his hands.

Then she looked at Seb and said, "Tell us what's about to happen."

And Seb did a big sigh and said, "**OK**. But you'd better sit down, Jodi.

This is **BIG STUFF**."

And I looked at Jodi and her face was all **SQUASHED UP** and I knew that it was because Seb was getting on her **NERVES** again because Jodi doesn't like not being the one in charge.

That's when Seb took an actual POCKET WATCH out of his jacket pocket and said, "We've got about three minutes. So listen up."

And that's when Zach started ⭐

⭐ ⭐ FREAKING OUT ⭐

⭐ ⭐

and yelling, "What's going to happen in three minutes? Does this have something to do with a MUMMY?! Because a MUMMY is how the curse got here, isn't it? ISN'T IT?! I need to go!" And he grabbed Maisie's paper bag and started breathing in and out really fast.

So Jodi reached across Maisie and put her hands on Zach's shoulders and said, "We're staying. We need to do this for Maisie, OK?"

And Zach sat back down and said OK. Then he started using the paper bag again.

Then Seb looked at his pocket watch and said, "Now it's two and a HALF minutes."

And Zach started breathing so DEEPLY that I was worried he might accidentally SWALLOW the paper bag.

That's when Jodi told Seb to hurry up and tell us what he needed to tell us.

And then Seb said, "So. I pretty much

know everyone here. You know that, right? And I know everything that there is to know about Ward 13. And maybe even the whole hospital."

I looked at Jodi and she had her eyes closed and was taking DEEP BREATHS through her nose which is a MEDITATION TECHNIQUE she learned after the time she screamed at Gary Petrie for breaking her ruler and got sent to the head teacher to learn about

ANGER MANAGEMENT.

So that's when I reminded Seb that we only had **TWO MINUTES.**

And Seb said, "Well, there's a **SANDWICH LADY** who comes to visit Ward 13 every day at lunchtime."

And that's when Zach whispered, "She's not a **MUMMY**, is she?!"

And Seb shook his head and said that it wasn't the **SANDWICH LADY** that we needed to worry about and that it was her **ANCIENT TROLLEY.** And that the trolley was so **OLD** that he thought it might be the **ACTUAL TROLLEY** that they used to bring the **MUMMIES** into the hospital for

RESEARCH hundreds of years ago.

Then Seb raised his EYEBROWS and gave me a LONG LOOK and he didn't blink for ages. And then he did the same to Zach. And then to Jodi.

And then he said, "I think THAT'S how the curse got here to Ward 13. I think it hitched a ride on the ANCIENT TROLLEY looking for fresh bandages to jump on because it LOVES living in bandages. And there's always LOADS of bandaged ARMS and LEGS and stuff in this ward because of people falling off their trampolines and stuff.

"But the people keep having their

bandages taken off and the curse has nowhere to live again. So it has to go back to the trolley until a new victim comes in. Like Maisie.

"And there's **MORE**. I think it **CURSES** the **SANDWICHES**, too! Because there's only ever **ONE** cheese sandwich and **LOADS** of tuna."

And then Seb gasped and said, "I bet it actually **CONTROLS** the sandwich lady through the trolley and makes her go the way it wants to go when it sees some **FRESH BANDAGES**. Then it **MAKES** her give the victim a tuna sandwich as a **SIGN**. I think it's

been jumping about this ward, going from arm to leg for **YEARS**. And that's why all the bad stuff keeps happening in Ward 13, like the sprinklers going off and people's stuff going missing. Like Maisie's dolphin."

And that's when Jodi narrowed her eyes and said, "How did you know about Francisco??"

And I knew that it was because Seb had obviously sneaked up on us again and overheard our secret meeting through the curtain.

But then all of a sudden Seb said, "**SSSSSSSHHHHHH!** Do you hear that?"

So I held my breath and listened and that's when I heard a SQUEAKY sound in the distance and my heart started beating MEGA FAST.

And I GASPED and Seb said, "That's the trolley. She's coming."

That's when Zach said that he thought we should keep the curtain CLOSED FOREVER. So I got Maisie's PAPER BAG again and held it up to his mouth and told him to BREATHE because he looked a bit PALE and also because he couldn't hold it up himself because he was sitting on his hands.

And then Seb leaned forward and took a **DEEP BREATH** and said, "**WHATEVER** you do, don't let her give you a **TUNA SANDWICH**. Or you'll be

DOOMED!"

Then all of a sudden the squeaking got **LOUDER** and Seb whispered, "Shhh! She's coming this way!"

We all listened as the squeaking got **CLOSER** and **CLOSER** until it was coming from **RIGHT BEHIND THE CURTAIN**.

And then all of a sudden the noise stopped and we saw a **SHADOW** behind the curtain.

And we all held our **BREATH**.

Because it was the **ANCIENT TROLLEY**. And it had **LOADS** of sandwiches on it!

A CURSED Sandwich

My heart was beating so hard in my chest that I could actually hear it. And I'm pretty sure I could hear Zach's too!

Then all of a sudden a voice said, "Can I come in, dears?"

And Seb looked at Jodi and Jodi nodded

so Seb said, "Yes."

And that's when the curtain SWISHED open and the sandwich lady stood there, smiling creepily and holding out a sandwich, and we all GASPED and Zach SCREAMED into the paper bag and it BURST and the bang woke Maisie up.

And then MAISIE started screaming because ZACH was screaming and the sandwich lady looked SHOCKED.

So that's when Seb jumped up and said that we didn't want any of her sandwiches of DOOM and the sandwich lady got a REALLY WEIRD look on her face and just sort of stood there STARING at Maisie while she was screaming and that's when we KNEW that Seb was right about the curse CONTROLLING her.

Then Seb pulled the curtain closed and Zach stopped screaming and I put Maisie's headphones on her and she stopped screaming too.

We all STARED at the gap between the curtain and the floor because we could see

that the
CREEPY CURSED
TROLLEY
was still there.

And then eventually it moved and the squeaking started again. We all sat frozen to the SPOT and nobody said a WORD until the squeaking got quieter and quieter until we couldn't hear it any more.

Then Seb said, "She's gone."

And I let out a HUGE sigh of RELIEF. I looked at Jodi and her eyes were WIDE and I knew that it was because she was thinking about Seb and how he knew so much about the ancient trolley and the tuna sandwiches of DOOM.

And that's when I realised that if I didn't ask Seb RIGHT NOW why he was in hospital all the time I probably never would so even though it probably wasn't the right time because of all of us nearly being cursed by a SANDWICH and everything, I said, "Seb. What's wrong with you?"

And Seb got a REALLY weird look on his face and said, "WHAT? Nothing! Why?"

And I said, "Sorry. I mean, why are you in hospital?"

And that's when his face went a bit red and he said, "Um."

But then he didn't say anything else after that.

That's when Jodi gave me a LOOK as if to say that I shouldn't have ASKED and that it was RUDE.

But then a little voice said, "Seb's got eczema and it gets really bad sometimes and he has to stay in hospital for a while so the doctor can treat it and make it better."

Maisie had taken off her headphones and was listening to us.

And then Zach said, "Is that why you wear

all the hats?"

And Seb nodded again and Zach said, "Cool. I like the one with the feather. Where did you get it?"

And Seb smiled and said that it used to be his granddad's and that his granddad was a MUSICIAN and that he used to be famous and in a band and everything.

And I realised that the suit jacket and pocket watch must have been his granddad's too.

And I looked at Jodi to see if she was going to say anything to Seb but she didn't. But I did notice that she was sort of STARING at him which was a bit weird.

Then all of a sudden Maisie started

SHAKING
VIOLENTLY.

And then she said, "What's that?!"

And I looked and saw that Maisie was pointing at the floor.

And that something had been slipped under the curtain.

And my heart almost STOPPED.

Because it was a SANDWICH.

And then Zach GULPED and said, "Please tell me it's cheese. PLEASE TELL ME IT'S CHEESE!"

But I knew before I even LOOKED that it WASN'T going to be cheese.

And I was right.

Because it was TUNA.

"HEY!"

Before I knew what was happening Zach jumped up and KICKED the tuna sandwich and it disappeared under the curtain.

And then someone shouted, "HEY! Who just kicked a sandwich at me?"

But we just sat in silence and didn't say

anything.

Then all of a sudden Maisie JUMPED a bit.

And then she said, "My leg's feeling WEIRD and ITCHY again. What if it's the CURSE trying to tell me more about FRANCISCO? Read it. READ IT!"

So we all looked at Maisie's cast and she made us check the bits she couldn't see over and over again. But there weren't any new messages.

That's when Zach said that it probably took HOURS for the message to SEEP through the cast because the cast was so SOLID and that there would probably be a message later on that night. And Seb said that he thought Zach was RIGHT and that there would probably be a new message from the curse on Maisie's leg cast in the morning and that we should all make sure we came back tomorrow morning to read it and keep doing the INVESTIGATION and bring him some grapes too.

But then before we could say anything else someone opened the curtain. And it was a nurse and she was holding a TUNA SANDWICH in her hand and she looked annoyed.

So that's when Jodi said that it was time to

go and the nurse said that that was a good idea and I knew that she'd said it because of all the GASPING and SCREAMING and KICKING SANDWICHES about the ward.

Then the nurse said that the doctor was on his way to see Maisie and also that her mum was waiting to see her because you're only allowed three visitors at a time.

So we said goodbye to Maisie and told her that we'd see her the next day and she did a BRAVE FACE and told us not to worry and also that Seb would be here all night and he looked at us and did a SALUTE and it made me feel better to know that he was in the bed across from Maisie in case anything else happened with the

CURSE while we were gone.

The next day when we arrived at the ward, Seb was sitting at Maisie's bedside with a NOTEPAD and Maisie was talking and he was nodding LOADS and writing down everything Maisie said.

And that's when Jodi put her hands on her

HIPS and asked Seb what he was doing with the

OFFICIAL
INVESTIGATION
NOTEPAD

and that's when I realised that it was JODI'S pad Seb was writing in and that she must have left it there by mistake.

That's when Maisie explained that loads of **WEIRD THINGS** had been happening since we were there yesterday and that Seb had offered to write it all down and get on with the **INVESTIGATION** until we arrived.

Then Seb said, "I tried to read all the notes in here to catch up but the writing's a bit messy."

I looked at Jodi and she looked **FURIOUS**. And I knew that it was because Seb had read our **OFFICIAL NOTES** without **PERMISSION** and that she thought he was trying to **TAKE OVER THE INVESTIGATION**. And also because he'd said Jodi's writing was MESSY.

That's when Jodi said that she NEEDED THE ROOM and she looked directly at SEB when she said it. But Seb just sat where he was and didn't get up because he obviously didn't know what that meant. But me and Zach DID know what it meant because it's what Jodi says when she wants everyone who is not part of the OFFICIAL INVESTIGATION to LEAVE.

I knew that Jodi was about to

BLOW

so that's when I asked Seb if he would be able to get us all some squash and he jumped up and did another SALUTE and said that he DEFINITELY WOULD and that he knew where the GOOD squash was kept. And then he rushed off.

As SOON as Seb left, Jodi GRABBED her notebook and sat down on the bed next to Maisie and said, "Tell us everything."

So that's when Maisie told us that she kept waking up in the night because there had been WEIRD NOISES. And that the noises had been horrible SCRAPING and SCRATCHING sounds.

And then she said, "They sounded really CLOSE. But every time I woke and sat up the noises stopped."

Jodi started writing everything down really fast even though it must have already been written down in there by Seb.

Then Jodi said, "Maisie. Is there anything else you can remember? Did you see anything at all when you woke up?"

But Maisie just shook her head and said, "The nurses put the big light out at night but you can still see a bit. But I didn't see anything."

And that's when I noticed that Maisie's

183

hands were **SHAKING** so I sat down on the bed next to her and held her hand and told her that we were here now and that she didn't need to worry any more about the scary noises.

But then Maisie said, "What about tonight? What if the noises come back? What if it's the **CURSE?!**"

And that's when Jodi said, "You don't need to worry about tonight, Maisie. Trust me."

I didn't know what Jodi meant by that and I was just about to ask her when Maisie sat up and **STARED** at us with her big eyes and said, "There's something else."

And then Zach gasped and said, "There's another message on your cast, isn't there?"

And Maisie nodded.

And Zach said, "Where? Let us see!"

But then Maisie shook her head and said that she didn't want us to see it and I could see that she was really worried and even looked a bit like she had TEARS in her eyes.

I thought Maisie was going to say that the message was about FRANCISCO.

But then she said, "It's about you guys."

And Jodi's eyes went WIDE and she said, "Show us."

And that's when Maisie pulled the sheet

off her leg and pointed to a **BIG** message scrawled right up the side of her cast in **GREEN PEN** and it said:

STAY HERE AND KEEP THIS CAST ON FOREVER OR YOUR FRIENDS WILL BE DOOMED!

FROM, THE CURSE

And that's when Maisie started **CRYING** and saying that she would have to keep the cast on **FOREVER** and probably live in the hospital because her leg was the

BROKEN
LEG
OF
DOOM!

The Broken Leg of DOOM!

When Seb came back with the squash he took one look at Maisie and said, "What did I miss?"

And that was because Maisie had **FAINTED**.

So that's when I explained that Maisie had

shown us the message about having to keep the cast on or we'd all be DOOMED and Seb nodded loads and said that we needed to be SUPER CAREFUL because the curse was POWERFUL and that it might give us all a RASH or CHICKEN POX or even BEARDS if we weren't careful.

And then he said, "We need to make sure Maisie keeps that cast on and she should probably stay in hospital until we can figure all this out."

And then Seb gave us all a cup of squash and he'd even written our NAMES on the side of the cups like they do in a COFFEE

SHOP and said that it was because he knew how STRONG everyone liked their squash because Maisie had told him. And then he smiled and raised his cup in the air and said, "ENJOY!"

So we raised our cups too and I said, "Thanks, Seb."

And Zach said, "Cheers!"

But Jodi said, "OUCH!" and then she put her hand on her side.

That's when I jumped up and said, "Are you OK?"

But Jodi shook her head and said that she WASN'T OK and that her side was hurting a bit and that she wanted us to get a nurse.

So Zach went to get help and I made Jodi sit down and drink some water.

Then Zach came back with a nurse and the nurse took Jodi away.

And that's when Seb looked at us with WIDE EYES and said,

"The CURSE strikes AGAIN!"

The next day after school I couldn't believe that I was visiting TWO of my best friends in hospital. But I WAS.

And that was because **JODI** had been admitted to the same ward as Maisie for **SUSPECTED APPENDICITIS** because of her sore side.

When me and Zach got to the ward, Jodi was sitting up in the bed next to Maisie and I

could see that she was wearing a HOSPITAL GOWN like Maisie's and Seb's, and that she was using a LAPTOP and wearing her GLASSES which she hardly EVER does even though she's supposed to.

I got a little bit upset when I saw her because I was worried about her. And about Maisie. AND about the curse. And I was also worried about myself a bit TOO because I didn't want the CURSE to come after me next and give ME appendicitis or something worse like a BEARD.

As soon as Jodi saw us she waved us over to her bed and told us to shut the curtain.

Just then a doctor came and took Maisie away to teach her how to use CRUTCHES.

So that's when I said, "Do you think the doctor is going to say she can go home today?"

And that's when Jodi said, "I hope not!"

And I was a bit surprised when she said that because Jodi was the one who WANTED Maisie to go home most. But then I thought that the reason Jodi probably wanted Maisie to stay in hospital now was because she was there too. But I wasn't sure because Jodi was being a bit WEIRD.

Then Zach asked where Seb was and Jodi

looked up from her laptop and did a bit of a **SMIRK** and said, "Good question!"

I didn't know what Jodi meant by that but I knew that we were about to find out because Jodi had that **LOOK** in her eye that she gets when she's

UP TO SOMETHING.

So that's when I asked Jodi how she was feeling and how her side was and she said, "What? Oh, yeah. I'm fine."

Then Zach asked her if we could get her anything but she didn't answer. She just kept STARING at the screen.

So that's when I said, "Jodi, what's going on? Did something happen with the CURSE?"

And Jodi closed the laptop and looked up at us and her eyes looked WEIRD.

And that's when she said, "There's nothing wrong with me. I'm not unwell."

So I looked at Zach and he looked at me because obviously Jodi was in DENIAL because she was in HOSPITAL wearing a hospital gown and EVERYTHING so she obviously **WAS** unwell.

So that's when I said, "Jodi. Um. You've got appendicitis, remember?"

But Jodi just shook her head and said, "No. I've got **SUSPECTED** appendicitis and I got kept in overnight for

OBSERVATION.

Which meant I got to stay here in the bed **RIGHT** next to Maisie all night to make sure she was **SAFE.**"

Then Jodi looked up at me and smiled.

And that's when I **GASPED** because I

realised what was going on.

So I said, "You didn't!"

And Jodi nodded and said, "I did. And I know it's lying but this is SERIOUS."

Then Zach said, "What's going on?"

So that's when I whispered, "She faked it! She doesn't have appendicitis!"

And Zach gasped and said, "JODI! You can't do that!"

And I knew that he said it because his mum is a NURSE.

But that's when Jodi said that she didn't have a CHOICE and that Maisie NEEDED HER and that she couldn't leave her alone in CREEPY WARD 13 for another night by herself with the

WEIRD NOISES.

Jodi said that she'd made an INSTANT PLAN in her head the MINUTE Maisie had told her about the weird noises in the night. And that her plan had been to get admitted to hospital and stay awake ALL NIGHT to see where the noises were coming from and keep a close eye on Maisie's CAST.

And that's when Jodi told us to come closer. So we did.

And she said, "Something happened last night."

And Zach gasped and said, "Did someone give you a tuna sandwich?!?!"

But Jodi shook her head and said that there hadn't been any sandwiches, just a bit of toast and some milk.

And then she said, "But I **DID** see something."

And there was something about the way she said it that made my heart start beating a bit faster.

Then Jodi said, "It happened about midnight. Right over there."

And then she pointed to the curtain and even though we couldn't see through it I knew that she was pointing to the other side of the bay where Seb's bed was.

Jodi took a deep breath and then she said, "At first I didn't know what I was looking at. But then I realised what it was. And that's when I knew that the curse was definitely REAL. And a LOT more serious than we realised."

Then Jodi looked at me and I

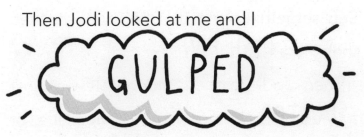

because I just **KNEW** that she was about to say something

and that it was going to change **EVERYTHING**.

That's when Jodi told us that she saw someone wearing a **LONG WHITE COAT** walk over to Seb's bed. And that he handed Seb something and that Seb took it, then they did a **HIGH FIVE**.

Then Jodi said, "I thought it was just a **DOCTOR** giving him his medicine or something because I couldn't see properly in the dark. But then someone else in the bay put their little bed light on and that's when I saw that the person with Seb had loads of BANDAGES wrapped round his head AND his whole FACE!"

And that's when Zach **GASPED** but Jodi said, "Wait. There's **MORE**."

And then she said, "Then a nurse walked past and the bandaged man **HID** behind the curtains until she was gone and then he ran away."

I looked at Zach and his mouth was **WIDE OPEN** and I wasn't surprised because this was

MEGA

WEIRD.

I had

NO IDEA

what was going on but then Jodi pulled
something out from behind her pillow and
said, "And then I found **THIS** over by the
curtain this morning."

And I looked and saw that it was a bit
of **BANDAGE** and it looked all **OLD** and
DUSTY.

And then Jodi looked up at us and said,
"Do you understand what I'm saying to
you?"

And me and Zach both nodded because
we DID.

There was a

MUMMY

loose in the hospital!

Maisie's
MUMMY
LEG!

Jodi said that she'd been reading ALL
NIGHT about MUMMIES.

And she thought that maybe there was a
MUMMY'S TOMB somewhere in the hospital
from when they were doing research on
bandages and someone must have found it

and set the mummy FREE.

Then she said that she'd found out that mummies were buried with loads of JEWELS and FANCY STUFF and RICHES and that if anyone stole any of their stuff they'd release a CURSE.

And I was in

TOTAL

SHOCK

because I hadn't actually thought there was a MUMMY loose in the hospital. I'd just thought that there was a CURSE left over from OLDEN TIMES. But this was a FRESH CURSE!

And then I remembered something and I said, "Wait. You said you saw Seb TALKING to the mummy? And giving it a HIGH FIVE?!"

And Jodi nodded and said, "I did. And I think HE was the one who opened the tomb."

And me and Zach both

GASPED.

That's when Jodi said that she'd been SUSPICIOUS of Seb since she first met him. And that's when I remembered the WEIRD LOOKS Jodi had been getting on her face when he was around and I realised that it probably WASN'T just because he was being annoying and that it was because Jodi thought he was up to NO GOOD.

Then Jodi said, "HE was the one who told us about the curse. And HE was the one who kept saying that we had to keep the curse trapped in Maisie's cast. Something just didn't feel right. He was DESPERATE for Maisie to stay here. Now I know why."

Then Jodi said that she thought Seb and the MUMMY were WORKING TOGETHER

because of the

MIDNIGHT MEETING

and the **HIGH FIVE** and that they **BOTH** wanted the curse to stay inside Maisie's **LEG CAST**.

And she thought Seb had found the tomb and **ACCIDENTALLY** released the mummy years ago when he first started coming to the hospital. And that he **OBVIOUSLY** didn't want to get **CURSED** so he tried to lock the mummy back in the tomb.

And then Jodi leaned forward and said,

"But I don't think the mummy WANTED to go back. I think it wanted to be FREE and so they

HATCHED A PLAN

together to TRICK the CURSE and get it to go into Maisie's LEG CAST so Seb wouldn't be cursed any more and the mummy would still be FREE. And I think the mummy is paying Seb in JEWELS and FANCY STUFF like the POCKET WATCH so that he keeps the mummy's secret."

But then Zach said that that didn't make

any **SENSE** and Jodi said that it **DID ACTUALLY**.

So that's when Zach said, "But why would the curse go inside Maisie's leg cast? Why wouldn't it just stay with Seb if he was the one who disturbed the tomb?"

And that's when Jodi crossed her arms and looked a bit **ANNOYED** and said that she didn't know the answer to that yet but that she **ONE HUNDRED PER CENT** planned to find out when Seb got back from wherever he was and she could do an **OFFICIAL INTERROGATION**.

And that's when I remembered the **LOOK**

on Seb's face when he saw how **BIG** Maisie's leg cast was and I gasped and said, "I think I know why the curse went into Maisie's cast! It thinks her leg is a **MUMMY!**"

And Jodi **GASPED**.

And Zach said that maybe we were **RIGHT** because even though the curse was in Maisie's cast, nothing bad had actually happened to her and the curse was probably just living in her **CAST** trying to protect her **LEG** because it needed a new home.

And Jodi nodded **LOADS** and said that that was probably why the mummy **HIGH FIVED** Seb because he was happy the curse had gone to live somewhere else because it was ITCHY like Maisie kept complaining about.

But then Zach gulped and said, "But that means that whoever takes off Maisie's cast when her leg's better is going to get CURSED."

But then Jodi said, "No. They won't. I have a PLAN."

And then all of a sudden a voice said, "I can hear what you're saying in there."

And we all GASPED.

I was NOT expecting to see Gary Petrie

when I pulled back the curtain. But I did.

Gary was standing there smiling and holding a big bunch of flowers and a **HUGE** teddy bear.

That's when Jodi said, "What are YOU doing here?!"

And I was just as surprised as Jodi because Gary Petrie is probably the MOST annoying person in our class (and probably even the whole SCHOOL) and he was the LAST person I thought would come to visit Jodi in the hospital because they are ALWAYS arguing.

That's when Gary said, "Where's Maisie?"

And then he looked at Jodi and said, "Why are you sitting in bed?"

So we explained that Maisie was with the doctor and that Jodi was in hospital now too.

And that's when Gary said, "Oh. Um. I didn't know."

And then he pulled ONE flower out of the big bunch that he'd obviously got for Maisie and handed it to Jodi and said, "Get well soon."

So Jodi said thanks and gave him a FAKE SMILE because the flower was OBVIOUSLY the smallest one in the bunch and it had even started to go BROWN.

Gary sat down on one of the chairs even though we didn't say that he could and then he said, "So. Where's this MUMMY you were all talking about?"

And   Jodi   gasped   and   said,
"SSSSSSHHHH!"

So that's when I knew I had to fix this FAST
because Gary Petrie is a

NIGHTMARE

and he'd probably end up ruining the

WHOLE
INVESTIGATION.

So that's when I said that we were just talking
about Jodi's MUM and how she missed her

and then I gave Jodi **WIDE EYES** and she said, "Yes. **YES!** I miss my **MUMMY** because I'm in hospital."

Gary **STARED** at Jodi for ages. And then he stared at Zach. And then at me.

And then he did a **REALLY ANNOYING** smile and said, "I don't think so. You're all **UP** to something as **USUAL**."

But then before he could say anything else, Maisie appeared with a nurse and she was walking with **CRUTCHES**.

Gary Petrie **JUMPED** up when he saw her and gave her the flowers and the huge teddy and almost knocked her over.

The nurse started laughing a bit and I wasn't sure if it was because Gary Petrie was wearing a SUIT with a tie and everything but I thought it might be and I had no idea why he was so dressed up to come to the hospital.

The nurse helped Maisie to sit down and then she said that she'd find a place for the flowers. And then she looked at the

GIANT TEDDY

and SIGHED and I knew that she was annoyed because it meant that Maisie had

even **MORE** stuff now.

Maisie looked a bit shocked to see Gary but she looked happy about it too. And that's when I remembered that they were sort of friends now after the school camping trip and the missing sausages and the **WEREWOLF**.

Maisie thanked Gary for the flowers and said that she **LOVED** the teddy and then she started to get tears in her eyes and Gary looked really

PLEASED WITH HIMSELF

because he obviously thought that Maisie

was crying because she loved the teddy so much. But I knew that it was probably because she missed FRANCISCO.

Then all of a sudden Seb appeared and I almost jumped out of my SKIN.

I looked at Jodi and she did WIDE EYES at me.

And that's when I saw that Seb had a STRANGE LOOK on his face.

And then he looked at Maisie and then looked at Gary and then said, "Oh. Hello."

And Gary looked up and said, "Hey. Nice watch."

And I saw that Seb was wearing a huge

fancy **GOLD WATCH** on his wrist.

And Seb said, "Thanks. It's an antique. It's worth

ONE MILLION POUNDS."

And Gary laughed a bit because he obviously thought Seb was **JOKING**. But I wasn't so sure after what we'd just found out about all the **TREASURES** that you get inside a **MUMMY'S TOMB**.

Then Gary asked Maisie if she would be coming back to school soon and if she would be bringing her **CRUTCHES** with her and I

knew that he specifically asked about the crutches because he wanted to TRY them.

And that's when Seb got a REALLY WEIRD look on his face and he said, "Just because you get crutches doesn't mean you get to go home. Maisie might have to stay here for AGES."

And then Maisie's eyes started to get all WATERY and she said, "I won't be going anywhere without Francisco."

And that's when the nurse came over and she said, "OK. There's too many people crowding around one bed here."

So that's when Gary said that he needed

to go anyway because his mum was waiting outside the ward for him.

And then he leaned over and took Maisie's hand and gave it a KISS and Zach laughed and Jodi made a BEING SICK sound. But Maisie just smiled and did a bit of a giggle.

And then Gary looked at me and said, "Izzy. Walk me out?"

And I had no idea why he needed me to walk him out because the door was right there and it wasn't like it was HIS leg that was broken or anything.

But I just went anyway because of what the nurse had said.

And then when we got to the door, Gary turned to me and said, "Who's the weird dude?"

And for a second I didn't know what he was talking about and then I realised that he must mean Seb.

But then he said, "I don't like him. And I don't trust him

ONE BIT."

The Ancient Mummy's Tomb

The minute we got to the basement I knew that this was a BAD IDEA.

We all stood in SILENCE for a few seconds after the doors to the lift shut behind us.

And then Jodi said, "There's no one here. Let's go!"

So me and Zach followed Jodi into the dark basement because the plan was to find the **MUMMY'S TOMB**. Zach's face looked funny because he's so scared of **MUMMIES**. But Jodi said he had to be strong for Maisie and she was right.

Jodi said that if there was going to be a tomb anywhere it was going to be **DEEP** in the basement and that if we could find it that would be **STAGE ONE** of the plan **COMPLETE**.

And when I'd asked Jodi about **STAGE TWO** of the plan, she said that that was going to be a bit more difficult because **STAGE**

TWO was to CAPTURE the mummy and put it back in the tomb where it belonged. And that if we did that the CURSE might leave Maisie's leg because the mummy and the tomb were its HOME.

I had no idea how we were going to CAPTURE the mummy but I was trying not to think about that and to just focus on STAGE ONE so that I didn't

FREAK OUT

because everything was starting to get a bit OUT OF CONTROL.

The basement was HUGE so Jodi said we should SPLIT UP to COVER MORE GROUND and that we had to be QUICK before the nurses noticed she wasn't just in the toilet like she'd said she was because they were already SUSPICIOUS about her FAKE appendicitis after she'd said that one of her symptoms was needing to eat more toast and biscuits.

So that's when I said there was NO WAY I was searching a creepy hospital basement for a MUMMY'S TOMB by myself and that I was staying with Zach and she nodded and said just to use the SECRET SIGNAL if we

needed her and then she ran off.

So me and Zach started searching for the **TOMB** but all we could see were rows of boxes and old medical equipment. But then we spotted an **OLD DOOR** covered in **COBWEBS** that said **MEDICAL LIBRARY**. So Zach turned the handle to see if it would open because it looked like it might have been locked for **YEARS**. And it did.

⭐

I was a bit scared to be the one to look inside first because the door looked **ANCIENT** and it had made a horrible **CREAKING SOUND** when it opened. And I had a horrible feeling

that if there was going to be an ANCIENT MUMMY TOMB hidden anywhere in the hospital that THIS was where it was going to be.

So I said that Zach should be the one to look inside first to make sure it WAS a library and not a room full of ANCIENT MUMMIES.

So he did. And that's when he said, "WOW!" and disappeared inside.

So I followed him and that's when I saw that he was RIGHT to say WOW because it looked like we'd gone back in TIME or something.

There were bookcases filled with old, dusty

books EVERYWHERE and little tables with old-fashioned LAMPS on them. And it looked like no one had set foot in there for ONE HUNDRED YEARS.

I took one of the books off the shelf and opened it and it was filled with DIAGRAMS of the HUMAN BODY and it was obviously from OLDEN TIMES and some of the pictures even looked HAND-DRAWN.

Then Zach said, "Come over here, Izzy. There's even MORE."

That's when I went over to the back of the library and saw loads of CRATES filled with even MORE books.

Zach said that he didn't think anyone used the library any more because loads of the books were probably OUT OF DATE because they didn't have all the new stuff about using MACHINES and COMPUTERS to help people get well.

I thought that Zach was probably right because there was dust EVERYWHERE and it didn't look like anyone had been in here for a really, really long time.

But then all of a sudden Zach GASPED and I looked to see what he was gasping at and that's when I gasped TOO because there was a huge CAGE in the corner.

That's when I started FREAKING OUT a bit and saying that maybe we should just GO because I didn't know why there would be a CAGE in an old library unless there was something that NEEDED to be kept in a cage so that it didn't get OUT.

But I knew that we needed to look and that we couldn't just run away (even though that's definitely what I wanted to do).

So I took a deep breath and said, "I'll go first."

And Zach nodded and I knew that I **HAD** to be the one to go first because I'd made him be the first one to go inside the library in case it wasn't a library.

And that's when I realised that when we split up, I should have gone with **JODI** because she's the

BRAVEST

out of all of us and I knew that if she was here that she would probably be INSIDE the cage looking around by now.

So anyway, I took a deep breath and walked towards the cage. But all I could see inside the cage were shelves with MORE BOOKS.

That's when Zach came over and he said that the books inside the cage looked DIFFERENT from the other books and that they looked like they were from even older ANCIENT TIMES.

And then he turned to me and his eyes were WIDE and his mouth was open even WIDER and he said, "What if the CAGE is

the mummy's tomb? And the books are part of its

TREASURE!."

That's when Zach said he thought that Jodi had been right and the mummy had been brought here **YEARS AGO** from **ANCIENT EGYPT** by medical researchers.

But then I said wasn't sure because I couldn't see any **JEWELS** or bars of **GOLD** or **BANDAGES** or anything like that.

And that's when Zach pointed to the padlock that was on the cage door and I saw

that it was OPEN.

And then he said, "Maybe there's more hidden inside. Only one way to find out!"

And before I could stop him, Zach opened the cage door and went inside and started looking around and TOUCHING THE ANCIENT BOOKS.

So that's when I said,

"What are you

DOING?!"

Because Zach was the one who'd said

that he knew LOADS about MUMMIES and MUMMY TOMBS so I couldn't believe he was going about

DISTURBING THINGS

because he was going to get

CURSED.

But Zach said that the TOMB was already DISTURBED and that the mummy AND the curse were gone so it was fine to touch stuff.

And then Zach said, "Come and see this."

And that's when we both **GASPED** because we spotted something **BIG** covered with a **WHITE SHEET**.

It looked like a big box or something but we couldn't be sure.

So that's when Zach stepped forward and **SLOWLY** pulled the white sheet off.

And that's when we saw that it was an old, fancy **CHEST** and I **GASPED** because I just **KNEW** that that must be where the **MUMMY** had been kept all these years.

Zach turned to me with his mouth **WIDE OPEN** and said, "If there's **TREASURE,**

then I'm telling you **THAT'S** where it'll be."

And I nodded because I knew that if we found even **ONE** jewel in the box then that meant we'd **DEFINITELY** found the **MUMMY'S TOMB**.

And when we managed to get the lid off, we both

Because there **WAS** something inside.

But it wasn't jewels or gold or even coins.

It was **FRANCISCO**.

Francisco Returns!

Francisco was COVERED in dust and he had a bit of a rip in his tail. But other than that, he was OK.

I couldn't BELIEVE that we'd found him and I knew that Maisie was going to be OVER THE MOON when she saw him!

Zach said that finding Francisco in here was **PROOF** that this was **DEFINITELY** the **MUMMY'S TOMB** and that we needed to go and find Jodi to let her know.

But then all of a sudden we heard an **OWL HOOTING** and we looked at each other and started to run because there was **NO WAY** an owl could have been down here in the basement and also because we knew that the sound of an owl hooting is our

SECRET SIGNAL

which meant that **JODI NEEDED US**.

We came **BURSTING** out of the library and ran towards the **LIFT** and when we got there Jodi was standing inside **WAITING** for us with her finger on the **HOLD** button.

And when she saw us she

GASPED

and said,

"WHERE?!"

And Zach yelled,

"In the TOMB!

We FOUND IT!"

And that's when Jodi said,

"SHHHHHHHHH!"

and then she pulled us inside and let go of the hold button and the doors closed.

Then as soon as we were moving Jodi said, "I think I saw it. The mummy. It was down there!"

When we got back to the ward I passed FRANCISCO to Jodi because I wanted her to be the one to give him back to Maisie.

And Jodi smiled and said thanks.

But then Zach said, "Um. I think you're in trouble, Jodi."

And that's when we saw that one of the nurses was standing by Jodi's bed and that she had her ARMS CROSSED.

That's when Jodi turned to us and said, "Just go with it, OK?"

So we nodded and that's when Jodi rushed over and said, "LOOK, MAISIE! WE FOUND HIM!"

And Maisie was SO EXCITED that she almost FELL because she was practising using her crutches.

Then Jodi turned to the nurse and said, "I was in the bathroom and when I came out Izzy here said that she thought she'd seen Francisco at the café."

And that's when the nurse looked at me and Jodi gave me a NUDGE and I said, "Oh. Yes. At the café."

And then Jodi said, "So, I was going to come back here and ask if I could go and help Izzy carry it but then Zach said that it might be GONE by that time and that we should just go RIGHT AWAY."

And then she nudged Zach and he said, "Yes."

And then Jodi said, "So we just all went right there and then and we all carried Francisco back because he's quite large!"

The nurse looked at Jodi and then at me and then at Zach and I just KNEW that she was thinking that that was probably the

she'd ever heard in her life.

But then Jodi said, "Look! Now Maisie

doesn't have to be upset or SCREAM any more."

And she looked RIGHT at the nurse when she said it. And that's when the nurse RELAXED a bit and unfolded her arms and said, "Well, less screaming would be good. I mean, it's good that you found him. And that Maisie's happy."

And then she said that Jodi needed to come and tell her if she was taking any more

TOILET TRIPS

and Jodi smiled and promised that she

would.

Maisie hugged Francisco for AGES and she kept saying, "THANK YOU! THANK YOU! THANK YOU!" over and over again to Jodi which made Jodi smile loads.

But then all of a sudden Seb walked into the bay and I saw that he was wearing a fancy jacket and that it had JEWELS on it!

Seb started to come over towards us but then he suddenly STOPPED and looked a bit like he'd seen a GHOST. And I knew that it was because he'd spotted FRANCISCO.

And that's when Jodi crossed her arms and said, "SEBASTIAN GOSS-CARLOS," and I GASPED because I had no IDEA Seb had such a fancy name and that Jodi actually knew it all.

And Seb gulped and looked down at the ground.

And then Jodi said, "Secret meeting. NOW. And YOU'D better come too."

And that's when Seb looked up with a confused look on his face because he obviously hadn't expected to be invited to the meeting.

Then Jodi pointed to her bed and we all went over and she closed the curtain behind us with a loud SWISH.

Then she told Seb to take a seat on one of the plastic chairs and she got up on to the bed and pulled the little booklight down and pointed it RIGHT at Seb so that the light was shining in his eyes.

And then she said, "We're going to ask some questions and we'd like you to tell us the TRUTH. Do you understand?"

And Seb nodded.

And then Jodi said, "Sebastian Goss-Carlos. Did you kidnap Francisco?"

And Seb said, "Yes. I'm so sorry, Maisie. I had to!"

And Maisie GASPED.

And then Jodi said, "Was the reason that you HAD TO because you are DESPERATE to keep Maisie here and that you thought if you hid Francisco that Maisie would stay here in the hospital until she found him?"

And Seb nodded.

And Maisie looked SHOCKED.

And then Jodi said, "And it was YOU who wrote the messages on Maisie's cast using the SAME green pen that you used to write on our squash cups, wasn't it?"

And I GASPED because I hadn't noticed that but Jodi was RIGHT.

And Seb nodded.

And Jodi said, "I suspected that it was

you doing the messages when you called Francisco a DOLPHIN because that's what was written on the ransom note too."

And that's when MAISIE grabbed the reading light and held it even CLOSER to Seb's face and said, "And it was YOU making all the scratching and scraping sounds at night, wasn't it? You were writing messages on my LEG!"

And I looked at Jodi and she looked at me because Maisie had just solved the mystery of the NIGHT-TIME SOUNDS.

And then Seb said, "Yes, it was me. I didn't want you to leave!"

And then Jodi said, "And is the reason you didn't want Maisie to leave because you made a deal with the MUMMY that you accidentally released when you disturbed the tomb in the hospital basement?"

And that's when Seb looked REALLY shocked and he didn't say anything and we knew that it was because HE knew that WE knew about the

and that he hadn't been expecting that!

And Jodi said, "I saw you with the mummy

last night. He was giving you a bit of his **TREASURE** because you let him stay free, wasn't he? That's why you gave him a **HIGH FIVE**. He probably gave you that **WATCH** you're wearing today."

And Seb looked down at his watch but he didn't say anything.

And then Jodi said, "And **YOU** didn't want to be cursed for life for disturbing the tomb and you knew that the curse had to go **SOMEWHERE** so you made it go inside Maisie's leg because it looks a bit like a **MUMMY**, didn't you? You're working with the mummy!"

And then Seb got a REALLY WEIRD look on his face and then he said, "YES. Yes, that's all correct. I'm working with the mummy."

And that's when Maisie walked towards Seb. And it took AGES because she wasn't very good at using her crutches yet. And when she eventually got there she leaned in close to his face.

And then she said, "No. You're not. You work for US now. Got it?!"

And I was **SHOCKED** and I could tell that Jodi and Zach were **TOO** because of the looks on their faces. Because we had never **SEEN** this side of Maisie before! And I knew that it must be because Maisie didn't like being **LIED** to by a **NEW FRIEND** and also because friends don't kidnap each other's **HUMPBACK WHALES**.

And that's when Seb sat up straight and said, "Got it."

Mission
MUMMY!

Jodi closed the curtains and made us take off our shoes and put them on the floor close to the edge of the curtain so it looked like we were still standing in them. But we weren't. Because we'd all sneaked out of the ward and were hurrying down the corridor in our socks.

Because we were on our way to find the **MUMMY** so we could put him back in his **TOMB** and get the **CURSE** out of Maisie's **LEG**.

Seb said that he knew somewhere that the **MUMMY** might be **LURKING** and that's when Jodi said that he needed to take us there

And that he was going to help us get the mummy into the **LIFT** and down to the

BASEMENT so that we could get it back into the TOMB.

Seb said that he would TRY but that it wouldn't be easy because the mummy DEFINITELY wouldn't want to go back in its TOMB and that it might take DAYS or even WEEKS to convince it.

And that's when Maisie held up one of her CRUTCHES and POINTED it at Seb and said that he was going to make it happen TODAY and that MUMMIES shouldn't be running LOOSE around a hospital with DIRTY OLD BANDAGES falling off them and that it was UNHYGIENIC.

So that's when Seb nodded LOADS and I giggled a bit because it was quite funny seeing Maisie look so angry and pointing her crutches at people. But then Maisie gave me a LOOK and I stopped giggling right away because I didn't want her to point her crutches at me.

That's when Seb yelled, "Follow me!"

And then he ran ahead of us.

So Jodi yelled, "Hey! Slow down!" because Seb was running too fast for us to keep up with him because Maisie was using her crutches.

But Seb DIDN'T slow down. He actually

started to run FASTER.

And that's when Jodi gasped and said, "Is he trying to run away from us? I bet he's trying to warn the MUMMY!"

So I shouted, "JODI, GO!"

And Jodi started to run after Seb and that's when Maisie said it would be quicker if we carried her so me and Zach took an arm and a leg each and Maisie yelled,

"TAKE ME TO HIM!"

So we ran after Jodi along the corridor and around a **TWISTY** corner until we came to a big door that said **"DOCTORS' MESS"**.

We had no idea what that meant but Zach said that it was a DEAD END and that there weren't any other doors and that Seb and Jodi must have gone inside.

So we put Maisie back down and peeked round the door.

And it WAS messy inside because there were dirty coffee cups and empty sandwich packets and newspapers EVERYWHERE. And also loads and LOADS of old TRAINERS lying around.

But we couldn't see Jodi or Seb anywhere.

But then all of a sudden we heard someone say, "PSSSST!"

And we looked around and saw Jodi hiding behind a sofa.

So we ran over and Jodi whispered, "Get down! The mummy's in the toilet!"

I looked at Zach and he looked at me because we were both confused about what was going on and I didn't even know that mummies USED the toilet!

That's when Jodi pointed to the far end of the room and whispered, "Over there. You see that door. I think it's a toilet. Seb went inside and I heard him talking to someone. The MUMMY must be hiding in there."

That's when Jodi said that she'd found a SHEET and that we needed to throw it over the mummy when it came out of the toilet and then somehow get it out of here and into the LIFT.

And I thought that sounded like a

TERRIBLE PLAN

but before I could say that, Zach said it was

a

BRILLIANT PLAN

but that we needed to get CLOSER to the bathroom door by hiding behind another sofa that was closer to the toilet. And also that we should use the SHOELACES from the old trainers that were lying around to tie the mummy's hands and arms behind its back in case it tried to put up a STRUGGLE.

So that's when we all started to move closer and Zach told us to pick up as many TRAINERS as we could on the way and I was really glad that we were all in our SOCKS because it meant we could walk without making a sound.

But then before we reached the couch, the toilet door started to open and we heard Seb say, "YOU shouldn't be in here either, should you?"

And that's when the MUMMY walked out and I SCREAMED and started throwing the

TRAINERS at it because I'd never SEEN a mummy before and it looked SCARY.

That's when Jodi shouted, "IZZY!" because I'd just ruined the plan!

So I stopped throwing the trainers and tried to say sorry but nothing came out because I was in SHOCK.

Then all of a sudden the door behind us started to open and loads of nurses walked in and the mummy turned and RAN out of another door that we hadn't even noticed was there! And that's when Zach shouted, "FOLLOW THAT MUMMY!"

So we did. And Jodi GRABBED Seb by the

arm and dragged him out with us and we all ran down the corridor.

And we kept passing bits of old BANDAGES on the ground and I was starting to think that the mummy was DISINTEGRATING because it had been out of its tomb for too long or something.

But then the mummy disappeared around the corner and when we caught up we saw

that it was getting into the lift so that's when I shouted, **"ZACH! DO IT!"**

And Zach knew **EXACTLY** what I meant so he **RAN** towards the lift but before he could jump up into the air and do his **NINJA KICK THING** he slipped and went **CRASHING** into the wall.

So we ran over to help him and he said, "Sorry! It's the **SOCKS!**"

And that's when we all looked up and saw the mummy looking **RIGHT** at us from inside the lift.

And then the doors closed and it was **GONE**.

And Zach said, "We've lost him."

But then Jodi said, "No, we've not."

And then she pointed to the sign above the lift and it said, **"SERVICE LIFT – BASEMENT ONLY."**

And then she smiled and said, "We've got him right where we want him!"

Dr Sam

As soon as the lift doors opened, Jodi stepped out and said, "We know you're down here. There's no point in hiding. There's five of us and only **ONE** of you. And we both know that you're **ANCIENT** and starting to fall apart. It's time for you to give up!"

And that's when we heard someone LAUGH.

And I couldn't BELIEVE that the mummy was laughing at us!

Then a voice from the darkness said, "That was a bit cheeky! And also, you're not allowed down here. Please go right back to wherever you're supposed to be."

That's when Seb whispered, "I told you he wasn't going to cooperate. We'll never find him down here in the dark. Let's go back to the ward and have another secret meeting and come up with a new plan!"

And then the voice said, "Seb? Is that you?

Please go back to the ward right away!"

But Jodi said, "We'll go back once we've put you back in your TOMB and the CURSE is out of Maisie's LEG!"

And that's when the mummy stepped out of the shadows and lifted up his hand.

And I held my breath because he looked REALLY SCARY and I didn't know what was going to happen next.

But then the mummy pulled a string and all the lights came on and we saw that he was wearing a HOSPITAL GOWN and pyjama bottoms with CATS ON THEM and also a doctor's coat.

And that's when the mummy said, "What on earth are you talking about?"

And Jodi said, "We're talking about you being a MUMMY who's escaped from your TOMB!"

And the mummy looked at Seb and shook his head and said, "Seb. What are you up to now?!"

And Seb shrugged his shoulders and said, "Sorry, Dr Sam. It was just a game. They saw you coming to check up on me in the ward last night and giving me the new cream for my rash and the comics and sweets and they saw your bandages and thought you were a

mummy."

And that's when Zach said, "Who's Dr Sam?"

And the mummy said, "I **AM**. And I might be **ANCIENT** but I'm not old enough to be a **MUMMY**, thank you very much!"

And that's when the mummy stepped towards us and pointed to the **ID** badge on his white doctor's coat and we looked and saw a photo of a man who didn't have bandages all over his face.

So that's when Jodi said, "How do we know that's you? We can't see your face properly."

And the mummy laughed again and said,

"Look at the ears."

So we did and that's when Jodi said, "Oh."

And the mummy laughed again and said, "You don't see THAT every day, do you?"

And he was right because both the man in the ID photo and the mummy had one GIANT ear and one TINY ear so they were obviously the same person.

DR. SAMUEL SAM
CONSULTANT PAEDIATRICIAN

And that's when Seb looked at us and said, "I'm sorry. I lied. Dr Sam isn't a mummy. I just went along with what you said because it sounded like fun!"

That's when Maisie said, "So there isn't a MUMMY?"

And Seb shook his head.

Then Jodi said, "If you're a doctor, why did you sneak into the ward at MIDNIGHT and then hide behind the curtain when the nurse came in? And then run away and hide down here when we found you in the doctors' mess?"

And that's when Dr Sam sighed and said

that he **WAS** a doctor but that he was also **TECHNICALLY** a patient.

But Jodi said that that didn't make any sense.

So that's when Dr Sam said that he **WAS** a doctor but that he had broken his nose badly during a **VERY** competitive sporting event at the weekend and that it was broken in several places and that he'd put the bandages all over his head and face himself because there was a lot of

SWELLING

that didn't look very nice and that he didn't want to scare his patients when he was checking up on them. And that he'd come down to the store in the basement to get more bandages without the nurses catching him so he could put them on himself and not bother anyone with it but that he wasn't very good at putting them on by himself and that was why they kept falling off.

And that's when Zach said that he didn't sound like a very good patient and Dr Sam laughed and said that he wasn't. And that the nurses kept telling him off for not resting and for getting out of bed to go and check

on his patients because he was worried about them and that he had to do it when the nurses weren't looking. And that was why he'd run out of the doctors' mess when the nurses came in because they would just tell him off for not being able to rest and stop working.

And that's when Seb said, "You might not be a good patient but you're a very good doctor."

And Dr Sam smiled and said, "Thanks, Seb. I just want you to get better and back to school

ASAP!"

And that's when Dr Sam said that it was time to go back up to the ward and we said **OK**.

But just before we left, Jodi turned to Dr Sam and said, "What sport was it?"

And I knew what Jodi was doing and that she was trying to see if Dr Sam was telling the **TRUTH** or not because Jodi says that it's the

SMALL **DETAILS**

that criminals forget about and that's what helps the police catch them out.

And that's when Dr Sam turned away a bit and I thought he was about to RUN for a second and that it had all been LIES but then he whispered something.

And Jodi said, "Sorry, what did you say?"

And Dr Sam sighed and said, "Chess. It was a chess game."

And we all looked at each other because we thought he was going to say

WRESTLING or

RUGBY or BOXING

or something like that.

But before we could say anything else, he said, "I tripped. It's embarrassing. Let's just leave it at that, OK?"

And that's when Zach patted Dr Sam's arm and said, "Don't worry about it."

And I knew that Zach had said that because HE'D slipped upstairs when he was trying to do his

NINJA MOVES.

But then Zach stopped and said, "Wait. So does that mean you're **NOT** cursed if the sandwich lady gives you a tuna sandwich?"

And Dr Sam laughed and said, "Well, I think we'd

be cursed if that was the case because Sheila gives **EVERYONE** tuna sandwiches! That's usually all there's left on the trolley by the time she gets all the way up to Ward 13."

Then Dr Sam had a little chuckle to himself

and said, "Seb. I know you don't like tuna. I don't think anyone does, really. But please stop making up stories about Sheila. It's not her fault that's all she has!"

Then Dr Sam knelt down and put his hand on Seb's shoulder and said, "I know it's hard being here all the time. And I know you get bored. But you have to stop making up stories about people. Remember the time you told your friends in the ward that the phlebotomist was a VAMPIRE? That upset a lot of people, didn't it?"

And Seb nodded.

And then Dr Sam said, "And one patient

even rubbed garlic bread all over his arms and that made the whole ward smell for a week, didn't it?"

And Seb nodded again and then he said, "Sorry, Dr Sam."

I looked at Zach and he looked at me and I knew that we were both thinking the same thing.

So that's when I said, "There's no curse, is there?"

And Zach said, "What's a phlebotomist?"

And that's when Dr Sam said that a phlebotomist is the person who takes BLOOD from your arm to help you get better.

And Seb said, "No. There's no curse. I made it up."

And Maisie

GASPED

and said, "Why, Seb? **WHY?**"

And that's when Seb told us that he'd made it up because he liked Maisie and that he wanted her to stay in hospital as long as possible because she was really fun to talk to.

And then his face went a bit red and he

looked down at the ground and said, "And you like Monopoly and you make me laugh."

And that's when **MAISIE'S** face went even **REDDER** than Seb's had and I knew that that meant she liked Seb too and I realised that was why she was so **ANGRY** about him **LYING** and stealing her **HUMPBACK WHALE**.

And then Seb looked up at Maisie and said, "I'm really sorry, Maisie. I shouldn't have taken Francisco. But I did make sure he was safe! I kept him in the old library book cage where all the old, expensive books are kept because it gets locked at night and everything! That's where I go to read my comics by myself. Anyway, I really AM sorry."

And he DID look it.

Then Seb said that he'd wanted us to keep visiting Maisie, too, because we were the best friends that he'd ever had in hospital and that he'd been having a great time with us and that he didn't want it to end.

And that's when Maisie said it didn't **HAVE** to end because she was going to keep visiting him in the hospital when she got out.

And he looked

SHOCKED

and he said, "Really?"

And Maisie said, "Yes, really."

And Seb smiled.

Just Go With It

When we got back to the ward, there were **TWO** nurses standing at Jodi's bed and this time their arms were crossed.

That's when Jodi turned to us and said, "Just go with it, **OK**?"

But then all of a sudden the nurses saw Dr

Sam was behind us and they rushed over and told us just to go back to the bay and then they didn't say anything else after that because they were too busy telling off Dr Sam.

So that's when Jodi told everyone to come and sit round her bed and then she closed the curtains and looked at Seb and whispered, "It was YOU who set off the sprinklers, wasn't it? Not a CURSE."

And Seb nodded.

And that's when Jodi shook her head at him and said that that was SERIOUS and that this was a HOSPITAL and that she didn't

say anything in front of Dr Sam because she

didn't want him to get into

SERIOUS
TROUBLE.

And then she made Seb **SWEAR** that he wouldn't do anything like that ever again. And he promised that he wouldn't.

And then Seb leaned towards Jodi and whispered, "And I also promise not to tell anyone that you

appendicitis to get admitted on to the ward because **THAT'S** a serious thing to do too

and I don't want **YOU** getting into

SERIOUS TROUBLE."

And that's when Jodi's eyes went **WIDE**.

And she said, "How did you know?"

But Seb just smiled and said, "You're not

the only one who wants to be a

DETECTIVE

when they're older."

And then Seb leaned back and put his hands behind his head and said, "So ... does your

allow new members? Maybe you could all visit me here sometimes and we could have a

There are a  **LOT**

of strange things that happen here, you know. I could use your help solving some of them."

And that's when Jodi smiled and said, "Maybe we will then. And we'll make sure we bring our **OWN** sandwiches!"

And we all

BURST

out laughing.

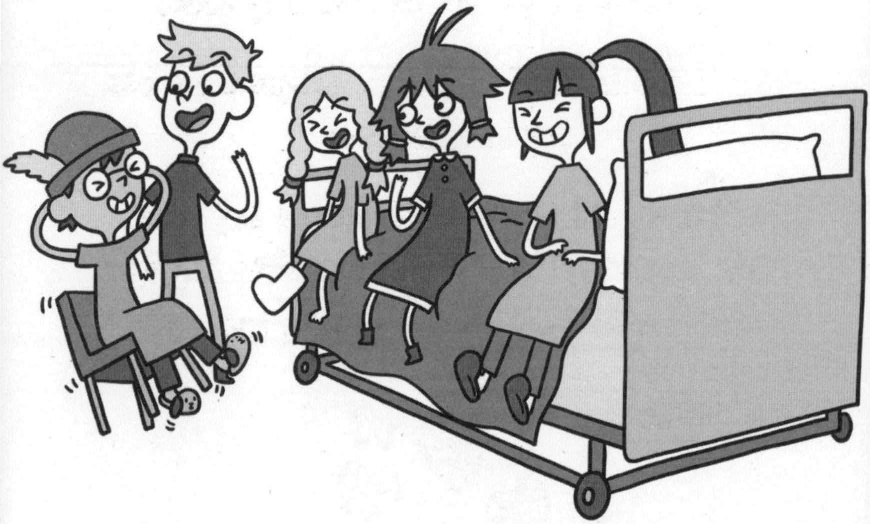

Acknowledgements

It was a bit tricky writing a book set in a hospital during a pandemic. I'd like to thank my editor, Kirsty Stansfield, and my agent, Becky Bagnell, for helping me try to get it right.

TOM! I know I say it EVERY TIME but I think this is my NEW FAVOURITE COVER! You are a genius. Thank you so much for all the time and hard work you put into the Izzy books.

Thanks also to Nic Theobald who designs the books. You. Are. Awesome.

And finally, I'd like to thank my wee boy, Albie. The original Extreme Dancer. You make Mummy want to write more and more books. I love you.

Another hilarious adventure with Izzy and friends!

MY HEADTEACHER IS A VAMPIRE RAT!

Read on for a SNEAK PEEK!

The Scariest Time EVER

I used to think that ghosts were the scariest things **EVER!** At our school we even have our own ghost, and she haunts the school dinners because that's where she died a hundred years ago when

she choked to death on the shepherd's pie. And now she haunts the dinner hall and the dinner ladies, but they still make shepherd's

pie. So I suppose she must not be that good at haunting people.

☆

Most people think it's only houses, and castles and schools that can be haunted but it's not; **ANYTHING** can be haunted. For

example, you could have a haunted shoe on right now and you wouldn't even know it. And there's not really any way to know for sure until your shoe flies off your foot or something. And then you know.

One time me and Jodi (that's my friend) found out that loads of stuff can be haunted when we were staying in a caravan with Jodi's gran, and Jodi's gran was sleeping, and Jodi was bored so she said, "Caravans are boring," and then all of a sudden Jodi's fold-away bed folded up with her inside it!

And I had to pull her out and it took ages because Jodi was tangled up in all the sheets

and she kept screaming,
"IT SMELLS IN HERE!
GET ME OUT!"

And then the next morning the toaster burned Jodi's toast. Then when Jodi was having a shower the water kept going hot then cold, then cold then hot, and Jodi kept screaming, and we both knew that the caravan ghost was annoyed at her because she'd said that caravans were boring. And it was obvious because all of the stuff was only happening to Jodi and not me, and not to her gran.

But this isn't the story about the Caravan Ghost, or about the Shepherd's Pie Ghost, or even about any ghosts at all. This is the story about the time that the weirdest and scariest

thing **EVER** happened. And it happened at our school.